'Why on earth should James think that . . .'

'. . . you and I are lovers?' Elliott asked softly.

Beatrice could feel the hot colour sweeping over her skin. Elliott knew quite well that she hadn't been about to say anything like that at all, and as she fought to get her embarrassment under control, she was amazed to discover that mingled with her anger was a fine thread of pain that came from the realisation that a man like Elliott could never desire a woman as ordinary as her.

Several times tonight he had introduced her as his new 'landlady', and she had been furiously aware of the interpretation some of her fellow guests had put on that description, but she was all too miserably conscious of how ridiculous she would sound if she tackled Elliott on the subject.

'Why is it you're so determined to provoke me?' she sighed instead. 'You force me to come with you . . . It's almost as though you actually *want* me to lose my temper,' she finished, perplexed.

He laughed softly and mocked, 'Got it in one, Bella Beatrice.'

SOME SORT OF SPELL

BY

FRANCES RODING

MILLS & BOON LIMITED
ETON HOUSE   18-24 PARADISE ROAD
RICHMOND   SURREY   TW9 1SR

*First published in Great Britain 1987
by Mills & Boon Limited*

© Frances Roding 1987

*Australian copyright 1987
Philippine copyright 1987
This edition 1987*

ISBN 0 263 75825 7

*Set in Times Roman 11 on 12¼ pt.
05–0288–49303*

*Printed and bound in Great Britain by
Collins, Glasgow*

CHAPTER ONE

ALL the way home from the interview her head was aching. She loathed driving in London's traffic at the best of times, and today, tensed up as she was with anxiety over the interview, her temples had started pounding almost as soon as she got into her car.

She was a nervous driver at the best of times, and as though other drivers sensed it they ruthlessly cut in on her, flaunting their superior self-confidence and skill in front of her aching eyes.

It was a relief to turn into the long drive of the house, a huge Victorian pile in Wimbledon with a massive garden. Her parents had bought it just before the twins were born.

Several other cars were pulled up untidily on the drive.

Even before she opened the front door she could hear the thud of pop music. As she turned the door handle and walked in, an adolescent male voice called out, 'She's home!'

The music stopped. Upstairs several doors slammed, and several pairs of feet thudded down towards her. Being left with the task of singlehandedly bringing up her four teenage siblings when only twenty-two herself hadn't been easy. Now, six years later, she was used to it, or so she told herself.

Sebastian and Benedict, the twins, came down first; tall, blond, and extraordinarily good-looking, at just short of twenty-one they dazzled the eye, even when one was used to it. Miranda was close behind them, eighteen, and as dark as her brothers were fair. William came last, glasses perched on the end of his nose, fair hair tousled.

There were times like this, when they surrounded her with their love and affection, when she would willingly have given them ten times as much as she had to take the place of the parents they had all lost.

There were others when she felt almost claustrophobic from the unending twenty-four-hours-a-day, seven-days-a-week responsibility that went with her guardianship of her four younger siblings.

No one, least of all themselves, had expected that two such brilliant and dazzling stars of the London stage as Charles and Cressida Bellaire would be so unceremoniously and unfairly deprived of life at the very peaks of their careers, and after the initial grief that had overwhelmed those they had left behind had come the appalling task of dealing with the financial chaos of a couple who had wholeheartedly and energetically put into practice their belief that life should be lived a day at a time.

Of course, had he known of his untimely death, their father might have had the forethought to provide for his families' future, but as it was . . .

They had been a celebrated and glittering couple, twice married to one another and once each to other partners, and their deaths had left a hole in the lives of their children and close friends that Beatrice doubted could ever be filled.

She was their eldest child, the child of their first youthful marriage. Impossible to imagine that her mother had only been eighteen when she was conceived. They had been divorced shortly after she was born—her father had been offered a prestigious contract in Hollywood, and her mother had balked at going with him, preferring to stay in Stratford where she was getting growing recognition for her own power as a Shakespearean actress.

Within a year both of them had remarried, her father to a rising starlet, whose name very few people, including Charles himself it seemed, had been able to recall to mind later, and her mother to a wealthy industrialist, fifteen years her senior, with a son of ten.

That marriage had produced Lucilla, her half-sister, the only child of the family who had not been blessed with a Shakespearean name. Ironically enough, it was Lucilla who had been Charles's favourite, for all that she was not his child.

Of course the press had had a field day over their second marriage. By then both of them were well known. After her second husband's death Cressida had returned to the stage, and on Charles's triumphant return from Hollywood to appear in one of the most ambitious versions of *Hamlet* ever put on the stage, it was inevitable that the two should meet again.

Their stormy relationship had all the ingredients necessary for high drama—and, Beatrice sometimes thought wryly, of a Restoration farce, but she kept these thoughts strictly to herself.

It wasn't that she hadn't loved her parents; she had—everyone had—but not even their most fervent advocates could deny that in many ways they had been irresponsible.

Even so, life without them had been darkly shadowed for a very long time, and not just financially.

Uncle Peter, her godfather and her parents' closest friend, had helped them, tracking down various royalties due from her father's films and pointing her in the direction of a careful bank manager and accountant. Fortunately the house had been paid for, and the unexpected bonus of a long-forgotten bank account had yielded sufficient funds to put the others through school.

Maybe it was because Lucilla looked so much like their mother that she had been Charles's favourite, Beatrice mused, as she tried to ignore her pounding head and sort out the garbled conversations battering her eardrums.

None of her siblings, it seemed, could stop speaking for long enough to let just one of their number have their say. They all had to bombard her at the same time.

Twin boys, then a daughter and then another son had been produced by her parents during their second marriage. They were the products of their most fruitful years, both emotionally and career-wise, and she loved them all. Like their parents they were confident and beautiful. Unlike her. 'The runt of the litter', as Lucilla had more than once mockingly described her. And it was true enough. She was plain—not ugly; just good old-fashioned plain.

Without the startling physical attractiveness of her siblings to throw her own lack of looks into relief she might just have got away with it unnoticed, but because she was a Bellaire... because she was a daughter of that famous couple... because her brothers and sisters were so undeniably physical replicas of their beautiful parents, her own lack of looks was thrown into constant prominence.

Only Lucilla was unkind enough to remark on it. The others, in view of their famed Bellaire outspokenness—also a gift from their parents—were amazingly tactful, not to mention protective of her. Painfully so at times, and in more ways than one, she recognised wryly, remembering the fate meted out to those men friends who had actually been daring enough to get past the front door.

'It isn't that we don't want you to get married,' Benedict had explained kindly to her on the last unfortunate occasion she had brought a man home. 'It's just that you haven't found anyone yet who's good enough for you.'

By whose standards? Beatrice had wondered a little bitterly. There had been nothing intrinsically wrong with the last one, Roger. He was a nice, quietly spoken man in his late twenties, who lived with his mother. She had met him in the library when he was changing the latter's library books. They had struck up a conversation, and their relationship had progressed slowly and tranquilly to the point where she couldn't put off the inevitable any longer.

She invited him home.

He had of course been completely out of his depth, and it was only when she hadn't heard from him in four weeks that Miranda carelessly admitted that he hadn't seemed too happy when she and the twins had explained to him that taking on Beatrice meant taking on them as well.

As well he might not be, she thought fretfully. Beautiful and multi-talented they might be; they were also a formidably daunting prospect to anyone not well acquainted with the Bellaire mental and physical energy and psyche.

'Nonsense,' her closest friend, Annabel Hedges, had expostulated when Beatrice put this view to her. 'Selfish, that's what they are. They know which side their bread's buttered on. You wait on them hand and foot, and you shouldn't do it. Turf them out, sell the house and make a life for yourself, Bea, before it's too late.'

How could she, even though sometimes it was what she longed to do? After their parents' death they had been so lost, so painfully dependent on her... Of course, then all three boys had been at boarding school and so had Miranda. Lucilla had just left RADA, and was starting out on her own stage career. But first Miranda and then the boys had pleaded and begged to be allowed to attend a local day school, and there had been the financial angle to consider, so she had given way. And once they were all at home they needed her there as well, so she had given up her catering course and stayed at home to care for them.

Today, though, she had made a bid for independence.

'Well, did you get the job?' Benedict, elder of the twins by ten minutes, grinned down at her from his six foot two height.

All of them were tall—apart from her. All of them had long bones and sleekly muscled bodies—apart from her. She was small and, while not exactly plump, quite definitely curvaceous. How she envied her sisters their slender small-breasted figures. Hers... She made a face to herself. Hers was definitely more along Earth Mother lines, she thought enviously.

Behind Benedict on the stairs, William scowled ferociously and addressed his eldest brother.

'What does she need a job for? We need her here, at home.'

'Yes, but you know Bea,' Sebastian, younger of the twins, put in mischievously. 'She does so adore a lame dog.'

'What's he like, Bea?' demanded Miranda, shouldering her brothers aside. 'Is he as absent-minded as Uncle Peter said?'

Beatrice had spent the afternoon supposedly being interviewed for the job of personal assistant to a young composer, who was a friend of her godfather's, but in fact, instead of being interviewed she had spent most of her time answering the phone and sorting out the chaos of unanswered post on the desk he had shown her.

'Yes to both questions,' she told them crisply. Her head was still pounding—tension, of course, and not caused entirely by her anxiety over the interview, or driving through the London traffic.

She had not forgotten last night's row with Lucilla. Unlike the others, Lucilla was not under her guardianship because she had been over eighteen at the time of their parents' death.

Beautiful, wilful, always antagonistic towards her elder sister, and financially independent, she had nevertheless chosen to remain in the family home, but now it seemed she had changed her mind. She had announced last night that she intended moving out of the Wimbledon house and in with her latest boyfriend.

Fair-mindedly, Beatrice had to admit that Lucilla had a right to her own privacy and that she was, additionally, old enough to make her own decisions, but her latest boyfriend was an aging television producer, already three times married, and with a particularly unsavoury reputation. Lucilla had tossed her blonde head and scowled bitterly when Beatrice had pointed this out.

When backed into a corner, Lucilla was always at her most dangerous and last night had been no exception. Beatrice felt as though she still bore the scars—hence the headache.

'I'm glad you're back,' William commented plaintively. 'I'm starving!'

William was the clever one, destined for Oxford, or so his school said, and as heartbreakingly handsome as the rest of the clan, although he preferred not to think so. Unlike the others, William was not intent on making a career for himself in the world that had once been their parents'; he had his sights set on other goals. Now, though, like any other seventeen-year-old, he was more concerned with his empty stomach than his potentially glittering academic career.

An expectant silence followed his announcement and Beatrice felt her spirits plummet as she observed the four pairs of waiting eyes. The task of finding and then keeping staff to run the huge Victorian house and its gardens was a constant thorn in her side.

No sooner was someone suitable found and installed than for one reason or another they decided to leave. Mrs Meadows had been with them less than three months.

'Where's Mrs Meadows?' she asked sinkingly.

'She got angry because Lucilla told her she was bringing some people round for dinner,' Miranda told her carelessly. 'So Lucilla told her she was fired.'

It was only with the greatest effort that Beatrice was able to hold back the words springing to her lips. With magnificent fortitude she managed a weary, 'I see.'

Obviously her words conveyed more than she allowed herself to say, and just as obviously she had not yet had the full budget of bad news. All the Bellaire offspring, apart from herself, were natural and effective hams. And, as the saying went, she could see from their faces that they were big with news.

'Well, what is it?'

It was left to Miranda to produce the scrawled note.

'Lucilla said to tell you that they'll be here at half past eight. She wants you to make your salmon mousse for starters, and then she wants that lamb thing that you do with the apricot stuffing, and then raspberry pavlova. She said to tell you that it was terribly important to make a good impression, so could you make sure that the silver's polished and that you use the Waterford glasses.'

Controlling her temper, Beatrice muttered under her breath, 'If it was that important, why didn't she take them out to dinner?'

Unlike the rest of them, Lucilla was comparatively well off. Her father had left her some money—a trust fund which was administered by her brother, Elliott Chalmers.

Already eighteen when his stepmother remarried her former husband, Elliott, on the verge of departing for Oxford, had remained, like herself, outside the charmed Bellaire ring, but unlike her he had not looked into it enviously. In fact, occasionally, watching Elliott watching her family, Beatrice suspected that she had detected signs of almost sacrilegious mockery, not to say impatience, in his cool grey eyes.

'Oh, and by the way, she's bringing Elliott with her,' Benedict put in with a grin. Beatrice's dislike and antipathy towards Lucilla's half-brother was a well-documented fact.

Beatrice herself felt as though she wanted to scream. Elliott Chalmers! That was all she needed! Of all the supercilious, bossy, domineering, sarcastic men, he really took the biscuit. She seethed bitterly as she headed for the kitchen, remembering how, after their parents' death, Elliott had advised her to keep the children in their boarding schools, warning her against landing herself with the responsibility of their welfare.

'They're my *family*!' She had thrown the words at him, her face flushed with temper.

'They're miniature vampires,' he had countered unrepentantly, 'and if you let them—and you will—they'll suck you dry.'

She had never forgiven him for his callousness, and she never would.

Alerted by the sounds coming from the kitchen, the four younger members of the Bellaire tribe retreated into the wings. Had anyone accused them of selfishness, they would cheerfully have accepted the accusation, but not really felt much guilt. They all loved Beatrice, but she was not like them. She was quite content with her life; she had no ambitions, no bright, luring dreams like their own. All of them took the security she had brought to their lives for granted, and, although they didn't know it, that they were able to do so was one of the most precious gifts Beatrice had given them.

She had been in her last year of a catering course at an exclusive private college when her parents had been killed in an air crash, and although all her dreams of owning and running her own restaurant had long since died, normally she still loved cooking.

Not today, though. She fumed inside as she set about preparing Lucilla's dinner party.

William, judging from the diminishing clatter of utensils that it was safe to do so, emerged into the kitchen and looked hopefully at her.

He would be wasted at Oxford, Beatrice thought wryly. With a talent like that he should have been headed for the stage. Even so, she found herself weakening and stopping what she was doing to make a perfect melting omelette, which he devoured with relish.

Long experience informed her that, while Lucilla expected her to prepare and serve food for her dinner party, she would not want her sister nor her younger siblings sitting down at table with her guests.

In spite of her beauty and her success as an actress, Lucilla was one of those people, always restless, never contented, who go through life defensive and envious of anyone they believe has something they do not.

Quite why there had always been a thread of antagonism between them Beatrice didn't know, but it was undoubtedly there. She knew that Lucilla resented her, but she could never understand why. If anyone, she ought to have been the one to feel resentful. After all, Lucilla had been Charles's favourite, not her. Lucilla had inherited the looks and the talent. It was her own guilt over that tiny seed of enmity that always made her go to greater lengths to appease Lucilla than she would have done for anyone else, but it never worked. Lucilla was relentlessly contemptuous of her.

At seven o'clock, with everything for the dinner party under control, she produced pizza and salad in the kitchen for everyone else.

William, despite his earlier omelette, ate almost twice as much as the others. At the moment he was tall and gangly, but in a few years' time he would have the same beautiful physique as his older brothers.

Oddly enough Elliott, who wasn't as tall as the twins, being just under six foot, always somehow seemed to make them look smaller whenever he walked into the room. He dwarfed everyone around him with the power of his personality—and with his wealth, Beatrice thought bitterly.

Knowing that he would be here tonight was really the last straw. Her head was still pounding despite the tablet she had taken; it showed all the signs of progressing into a migraine. The smell of food almost nauseated her, and she longed to go upstairs and lie down.

'Aren't you going to get changed?' demanded Miranda when she had finished eating. 'You can't sit down to dinner like that. You know what Lucilla and her friends are like. It'll be designer dresses and everything that goes with them.'

Miranda was heavily into clothes. She was doing a course at college which she hoped eventually would lead to a career in theatrical costume design.

'Oh, come on, Mirry,' Sebastian cut in. 'You know our dearest Lucilla would never allow Bea to sit down with her friends. You shouldn't let her get away with it!' He frowned, looking so severe for a moment that Beatrice couldn't help smiling.

Of all of them Sebastian was perhaps her favourite: just a little less colourful than his elder twin, just a little less self-confident and consequently just a little less overpowering. He was the one she felt closest to. He came up to her now and hugged her.

'Poor Bea, we all treat you dreadfully, don't we? But despite it all you still love us, don't you?'

Oh, so easily they tied her to them . . . How many times after their parents' death had she heard those words? How *could* she have deserted them? How *could* she have been selfish enough not to care?

Very easily, if you'd been a true Bellaire, a surprisingly strong inner voice taunted, but she ignored it, quickly clearing the table and shooing them out.

A quick last-minute look at the dining-room showed her that Lucilla would not be able to fault a thing.

The dining-room was at the back of the house overlooking the gardens, lush now with early summer promise. The Hepplewhite table and chairs, discovered by her mother and bought for a song, gleamed richly in the evening sunshine. Snowy white linen napery, glittering crystal, shining silver. A bowl of fruit carefully frosted to look decorative added a touch of colour. She hoped Lucilla had remembered the wine.

After dinner, Lucilla would want to take her guests into the small drawing-room for coffee. Beatrice hurried into it, gritting her teeth against the pain as she rushed round picking up belongings carelessly scattered on the chintz-covered sofas. This room too overlooked the gardens, but on two sides instead of one. It was a warm, gracious room, and only this morning she had filled it with freshly cut flowers.

In the hall the grandfather clock chimed. Eight o'clock. Where had the time gone?

In the kitchen all was in order, but the heat from the oven brought a flush to her creamy skin. Her fine brown hair had escaped from its confining knot and was curling wildly round her face. She knew from experience that her nose would be shiny and that her soft hazel eyes weren't as large or as lustrous as the magnificent dark blue orbs inherited by the rest of the family. A throwback, her mother had once laughingly called her. At the time it had hurt, but she had learned to smile and be grateful for what she *did* have. After all, it was scarcely her parents' fault that she wasn't like them . . . that she wasn't a beautiful Bellaire.

She heard a car and then another, and wiped her hands before walking into the hall.

'Ah, there you are . . .'

Tall and impossibly beautiful, Lucilla was glittering with malice as she swept in, her friends at her heels. Beatrice felt her heart sink. She knew Lucilla in these wild, almost dangerous moods.

Tonight her sister was dressed in dark pink silk, a perfect foil for her colouring and a clever choice. It made the other women in the party, both brunettes, fade into insignificance.

Lucilla had her arm draped through that of her companion, and Beatrice's heart sank even further as she recognised the TV producer and the challenge in Lucilla's eyes.

'Elliott darling, where are you with that wine?' she called over her shoulder.

Elliott brought up the rear of the party. Like the other men he was wearing a dinner-suit, but as always he seemed to dwarf the others with his presence. Without moving a muscle he somehow managed to convey an adult forbearance of the antics of other, lesser mortals.

It was that air of insufferable superiority about him that always infuriated her so much, Beatrice decided as Lucilla passed her the wine with one hand and waved the other to her friends, indicating that they should hand her their coats.

'Still playing the Martha, are we, Beatrice?' Elliott murmured to her as he handed her his. 'You really ought to go for another role, my dear. This one's getting rather wearing, although I must admit at times it becomes you.'

Beatrice could feel hot blood scorching her skin as she fought against her anger. Stiff-backed, she took the coats into the cloakroom.

Lucilla hadn't introduced her to her friends, but then she never did. More than any of the others, Lucilla enjoyed being a Bellaire. She had even changed her surname from Chalmers to Bellaire. Beatrice risked a glance at Elliott and wondered sardonically how he had liked that. Although he had never expressed it, she sensed it was his opinion that a Chalmers was superior to a Bellaire any day of the week.

Yes, of all of them, Lucilla was the one who clung the most to their parents' memory and reputation. She enjoyed being described as her mother's daughter, and there were even times when Beatrice didn't wonder if she would have preferred to be their only child, she was so fiercely possessive of her status.

By the time Beatrice had served the main course, her headache had worsened to such a degree that she could barely see. She took in the sweet, intending to tell Lucilla that she would have to attend to her guests' coffee herself, when one of the brunettes piped up gratingly,

'Lucilla my dear, you're so lucky to have such excellent staff.' She had a transatlantic accent which no doubt accounted for her lack of knowledge about Lucilla's family background, but Beatrice stiffened with misery and resentment as she saw the amused smiles touch other more knowing mouths.

As though he was a magnet, she found her gaze drawn to Elliott. He was regarding her impassively, drinking the last of his wine, his eyes taunting her over the rim of his glass.

'Oh, Beatrice isn't the help, Angela,' he drawled mockingly, looking at her. 'She's Lucilla's sister.'

The brunette's mouth fell open in shock.

'Oh, but she can't be . . .' she began, and the TV producer smiled dazzlingly into Lucilla's eyes and said with both relish and amusement, 'Oh, but she is. The runt of the litter, isn't that what you call her, darling?'

Later, Beatrice couldn't remember anything about how she got out of the room. Somehow she found herself back in the kitchen, its familiar surroundings swaying horribly as the pain in her head reached crescendo proportions.

It was no use pretending that their laughter hadn't hurt. It had.

Almost blinded by the pain in her head, she leaned her face against the cool wall tiles.

She supposed she ought to have expected something like this. Lucilla had been furious with her last night, and her friend's ignorance had given her an ideal opportunity to get her own back.

'It's your own fault, you know. You should learn to say "No" and mean it!' The coolly amused voice somewhere in the region of her left ear was the last straw. Elliott had followed her into the kitchen! Oh, he would ... he would! It was either scream, Beatrice thought bitterly, or burst into tears, and she didn't think she had the energy for the former.

To her chagrin, he turned her round. Elliott took one look at her tear-blotched face and burst out laughing.

'Now I've seen everything,' he told her unkindly. 'A Bellaire who doesn't cry beautifully. My poor Beatrice! You really *are* the cuckoo in the nest, aren't you?'

It was too much. To be reminded of her lack of looks, now, when she was feeling at her most vulnerable, and by this man of all men! She wanted to scream and rage. She wanted to pick up something heavy and throw it at him. She wanted ... She gritted her teeth and looked into his eyes.

Her own widened, and she stared at him blinking. He was looking at her with a mixture of encouragement and amusement as though ... as though he *wanted* her to lose control. But why?

It was the final, but the final straw.

She launched herself at him like a small spitting cat, and would have raked her nails down his face if he hadn't stopped her by gripping hold of her wrists.

'Hallelujah!' she heard him exclaim softly and inexplicably. 'But you know, my dear Beatrice, I can't let you get away with it—it wouldn't be good for you. A classic production, none the less, and that being the case...'

He moved, shifting his weight somehow, so that she fell heavily against him. His arms tightened round her, and she could feel the steady drum of his heart.

She looked at him in bewilderment. Her head was still pounding. She wasn't sure how she came to be in his arms or, more important, why.

He bent his head, his eyes silver grey and quite brilliant; her own widened as she realised that he intended to kiss her. She moved jerkily, but not quickly enough.

His mouth felt warm and surprisingly soft against her own. She could taste the wine he had been drinking. She felt dizzy... shaky and dangerously vulnerable. The sensation of his tongue-tip moving against her lips completely unnerved her. She was still trying to decide whether that was because she didn't like it or because she did, when the kitchen door opened and Lucilla walked in.

'Where's the coffee?' she began peremptorily, stopping abruptly as she saw Elliott holding Beatrice in his arms.

'Oh, my God, now I've seen everything! Elliott, what on earth are you doing? You must be hard up for a woman if you're having to resort to Beatrice! Honestly, she wouldn't know what to do with a real man—you should see the wet specimens she brings back here.'

With a tormented sound, Beatrice tore free of Elliott and raced past Lucilla, not caring any longer what anyone might think of her odd behaviour. She was past caring about that. She had never felt so humiliated, or so . . . so disturbed in all her life.

In the sanctuary of her bedroom she sank down into a chair. Her whole body was trembling.

Elliott had kissed her!! Elliott, who she well knew disliked and despised her; Elliott whom she loathed and detested; Elliott, who had made her forget, however briefly, that she was plain, and remember only that she was a woman!

She couldn't believe it . . . she didn't want to believe it.

She *would not* believe it!

CHAPTER TWO

THE next morning, for almost the first time in her life, Beatrice overslept. She woke up and stared in shock at her alarm, her brain still fogged with the tablets she had taken for her headache.

It was almost nine. Why had no one been to wake her up? Where was everyone? Panicking, she got out of bed and hurried into her bathroom, dressing quickly in jeans and a bulky sweatshirt. She always wore loose tops; they disguised the lush fullness of her breasts. She always felt uncomfortable about the size of her chest, aware that if she didn't wear something concealing men stared at her. She was too used to thinking of female beauty in terms of her mother and sisters to realise that, to some, her petite curvy shape was the embodiment of all their most private fantasies, and she would have been shocked had any of them told her so.

She could hear voices coming from the kitchen. At least everyone else had not overslept, although it was unheard-of for the rest of her family to even think about getting their own breakfast.

She pushed open the door and came to an abrupt halt. Sitting in the chair that had once been her father's was Elliott Chalmers.

'Good morning, Beatrice. Headache all gone?'

There was no sign of Lucilla, and the others were all watching her with varying degrees of curiosity.

'Why didn't someone come and wake me?'

'Because I told them not to!'

Her eyes swivelled to meet Elliott's, expressing their total disbelief.

'Isn't it time you went home, Elliott?' she demanded frigidly, clutching at the frayed remnants of her dignity. What on earth was he doing here? He must have stayed the night.

'Haven't you heard? This *is* my home . . . at least for the next three months. Lucilla invited me to move in when she heard about the problems I'm having with the contractors.'

Dimly Beatrice remembered Lucilla mentioning something about the work that was being done on Elliott's London apartment, but she had said nothing about inviting him to move in with them.

Anger burst into life inside her, and she longed to shriek that he was not staying, and that he could leave right away, but she knew that in an outright quarrel she had no hope of outwitting him. Elliott never lost his temper and was a formidable foe, as she well remembered from her teenage years.

'Thoughtful of her to suggest I stay here, wasn't it?' he continued with a cool effrontery that took her breath away.

He must have heard her indrawn gasp—there could be no other explanation for the gleam she suddenly saw in his eyes as he drawled, 'Yes, I knew you'd think so, Beatrice.'

'Stay if you want,' she said ungraciously. 'There's enough room.' That wasn't at all what she had intended to say, but it was too late to recall the words now.

The grey gleam deepened, making her suddenly feel acutely vulnerable for some reason.

'Most gracious of you.'

'Ah, but you haven't heard the house rules yet, has he, Bea?' Benedict teased, blue eyes dancing with amusement. 'No reading under the bed-clothes, Elliott—it's bad for your eyes...and for your spots—depending on what you're reading,' he added incorrigibly, making Beatrice flush scarlet as she remembered her long-ago words to her brother when she had caught him sneaking pin-up maga-zines into his room.

'No raiding the fridge at night. No drinking par-ties. No smoking—of any kind. And definitely no girls in your room after lights out. Have you told him that bit yet, Bea?' Benedict was grinning irre-pressibly at her.

'Ben,' she began repressively, but Elliott seemed unmoved by her younger brother's disclosures and merely said affably, 'Since I don't date *girls*, I don't think I'm going to have any problems.'

He stood up, brushing toast crumbs off his im-maculate pin-striped suit. This morning he looked every inch the successful businessman that he was and Beatrice reflected darkly that it spoke volumes for the Machiavellian character she had always sus-pected he possessed that neither of the twins so much as tried to get a rise out of him over his sober attire. Had any of the men she had infrequently dated appeared at the house thus dressed they would have been baited almost to the point of insanity. Like their parents before them, the twins displayed a cheerful irreverence towards anything even remotely Establishment. But it was as though Elliott was protected by his own invisible radar, and, what was more, they seemed to know it because they treated Elliott with . . . with respect, she acknowledged a little resentfully, recalling how often she had wished they might accord her that same virtue.

'Just as well you're not starting the new job this morning, Bea,' commented Benedict, lazily helping himself generously to the butter and plastering it on his toast. Without looking up from his task he added, 'Did you know that Bea's got herself a job, Elliott? Working for a famous composer, would you believe, or at least he will become a famous composer one day. Isn't that what Uncle Peter says, Bea?'

Her muscles still felt stiff from the pain of her migraine, and for some reason it hurt to force the calm smile with which she acknowledged her brother's comments.

She was conscious of Elliott watching her with the same unblinking intensity that a cat might watch a mouse. Already she was tensing her body against one of his mocking remarks, but when she nerved herself to look directly at him she saw that he had switched his attention from her to Benedict and, what was more, that the look the two of them were exchanging had for some reason brought a bright gleam of triumph to her brother's eyes.

That made her frown. As far as she knew, Elliott had always got on reasonably well with the rest of her family. *She* was the only one of them who disliked him.

'I suppose you know that Lucilla is leaving here to move in with her latest boyfriend,' Sebastian commented, and, as Elliott's attention switched from one twin to the other, Beatrice found she was expelling a faint sigh of relief.

She was a coward, she acknowledged wryly as she got up to make some fresh coffee; definitely one of the 'peace at any price' brigade, but why not? Not everyone could be a moral crusader, not just ready but eager to spring into battle at the slightest provocation. The twins, especially Benedict, thrived on conflict of any kind, and there was nothing Ben loved more than a stimulating argument, as she had good cause to know.

'She *is* over twenty-one,' Elliott pointed out.

'Well over,' Miranda added *sotto voce* to Elliott's calm remark, earning herself a frown from Beatrice, and the lift of one faintly querying eyebrow from Elliott himself.

'Even so, I don't think her proposed move is a viable one,' Elliott continued calmly, 'and I've told her as much. Of course she's a free agent, but . . .'

'But you control her purse strings,' Benedict put in a little crudely, adding, with a wicked gleam in his eyes, 'and sanctions could be imposed . . .'

Beatrice tensed, but Elliott refused to rise to the bait.

'Indeed they can,' he agreed, 'but sanctions, if indeed there are to be any, are a subject only for discussion between the concerned parties, if you follow me, Benedict. Which puts me in mind of another matter,' he continued, before Benedict could make any comment. He glanced at his watch.

'I don't have time to discuss it now, which is perhaps fortunate. I'm going to the city if anyone wants a lift. I'll be leaving in exactly fifteen minutes.'

Miranda stood up quickly, gulping down her coffee. This morning her black hair was arranged in a spiky halo around her face. Her lipstick was white, and she had stencilled a floral design around and beneath one eye.

Although she hated to admit it, Beatrice observed that the overall effect was unarguably attractive, but then Miranda would look good in a sack, and make-upless.

'Yes, please, I'd love a lift, Elliott.' She smiled winningly at him, the smile of a girl who had no doubt of her own attractions. 'Could you drop me at Covent Garden? I want to browse round the market stalls. I need some antique lace...'' Her smile switched suddenly to a frown. 'Oh God, I'd forgotten. I'm going out tonight and I was going to wear... Bea, will you be an angel and wash and iron my black dress for me? I think it's on my chair, or it might be on the floor.' She frowned as she tried to concentrate, and, knowing her sister's untidiness, Beatrice did not for one moment doubt that she was having difficulty in visualising exactly where she had dropped the obviously now all-important garment.

'I'm afraid Beatrice won't be able to do that for you, Miranda,' Elliott said pleasantly, without taking his eyes from the newspaper he was scrutinising.

He spoke quietly, but it was as though he had shouted out loud, as five pairs of eyes mirroring different degrees of shocked disbelief turned in his direction.

Miranda was the first to recover.

'Why?' she demanded baldly.

'Because tonight your sister is going out, and she'll be too busy washing and ironing her own dress.'

Miranda gaped at him. 'Beatrice going out! But she never goes out,' she claimed with admirable disregard for the truth.

'Never?' One dark eyebrow rose in amusement. 'I suspect that's an exaggeration, but I'll let it pass. I can see you're suffering from shock,' he added with avuncular kindness.

'You never said anything about having a date.' Miranda switched her attack, fixing hurt eyes on Beatrice's blank face. 'Who are you going out with?'

'Me,' Elliott interrupted calmly. 'Not that it's really any of your concern, my sweet selfish child, and since, as I've already pointed out, I shall require her to wash and iron her own party dress, it thus follows that she won't have time to do yours. Do it yourself, mm, Mirry?' he suggested, smiling at her. 'It won't hurt you.'

Beatrice wasn't sure which held her the most transfixed, his outrageous comment about taking her out, or the effect of that singularly sweet smile which had been directed at her sister, but which was having the oddest effect on her own senses.

Quickly pulling herself together, she opened her mouth to tell him in no uncertain terms that they most definitely did not have a date, when he strolled over to her, leaned down, and before she could stop him placed a brief kiss against her parted lips.

When she wrenched away from him, he apologised insincerely. 'Ah, obviously my mistake. I thought you wanted me to kiss you, Bea! Goodbye. Don't worry about it,' he added with kindly indulgence. 'It's just an automatic reflex, that's all.'

As he sauntered off through the kitchen door, he called back over his shoulder, 'Ten minutes, Mirry, otherwise I'm going without you.'

For a moment the kitchen fairly hummed with the intensity of the silence, and then Benedict looked speculatively at Beatrice and said thoughtfully, 'I wonder why he's taking you out, Bea. I wouldn't have thought you were his type at all.'

Beatrice already knew she wasn't. Elliott's taste normally ran to long-legged model-like creatures with haughty expressions and rather county-type backgrounds, but that didn't make her brother's comment any less painful to bear.

Before she could say anything Sebastian added appreciatively, 'I like his style, Bea . . . kissing you like that. Mind you, you did rather goggle at him. I wonder who he's in the habit of kissing goodbye after breakfast. He's rather a fastidious soul, our Elliott. As far as I know he's never had a live-in companion, has he?'

'I expect he normally sleeps over at their place,' Benedict responded. 'It would be much more economical that way, and you know how our Elliott feels about saving money.'

If she hadn't been so ruffled and upset Beatrice would have reminded her brother that he was being more than a little unfair. Elliott might not splash his money about in the theatrical fashion of their late parents, but he was far from mean, and always gave her brothers and sisters extremely generous gifts of money for birthdays and Christmas.

He never gave her anything, though. He probably felt, if indeed he gave any thought to the matter at all, that being adult she was beyond the age of meriting gifts of any sort. Not that she would have accepted money from him even if he had chosen to give it, but last Christmas at the family party they always had on Boxing Day both Mirry and Lucilla had sported expensive designer dresses bought out of the generous cheques given to them by Elliott. She had worn the old black velvet she had had for years—her one and only 'formal' outfit.

Stubbornly she reflected that, whatever Elliott's purpose in announcing that they were going out tonight, she was not going to go with him, and she would tell him so, tonight, when she hoped they wouldn't have an interested audience.

She heard Mirry racing downstairs, and then the slam of the front door and the sound of a car starting up.

'I love that new Jag Elliott's just bought,' enthused Sebastian as he poured himself a fresh cup of coffee.

'Yes, he's slipping a bit,' Benedict responded darkly. 'A sporty car like that doesn't fit in with his image. It betrays the fact that there's a lot more to him than meets the eye. Did you know he was going to be staying here?' he asked Beatrice almost accusingly.

'No, I didn't. Shouldn't you two be at the studio by now?' she asked, glancing at the kitchen clock.

The twins had both landed parts in a popular 'soap' series which paid well, although Benedict constantly bemoaned the fact that it was too trite for words and hardly qualified as acting.

'God, yes!' Sebastian gulped down his coffee. 'Come on, Ben, get a move on, otherwise Sam Johnson will be tearing a strip off us again!'

Sam Johnson had been a friend and contemporary of their parents and he was directing the production they were working on. Like everyone else, he tended to make allowances for the famous Bellaire temperament. For a moment a faint frown touched Beatrice's forehead. It was occurring to her more and more recently that too many people, including herself, made too many allowances, perhaps. She moved uncomfortably in her seat. It wasn't exactly that her brothers and sisters were spoilt, but just occasionally recently she had detected something in their manner to others that suggested a rather unpleasant sense of superiority. Quickly she checked the thought. She was becoming over-sensitive; she had Elliott to thank for that. He always made her feel prickly, and aware of the vulnerabilities and flaws in her family in a way that she always wished she could ignore. It was as though in Elliott's presence she saw them in a different light . . . almost indeed as though he deliberately incited them, especially Benedict, to reveal aspects of their personalities to her that she would rather have remained unaware of.

It was almost eleven before she had the house to herself and after twelve before she had finished tidying bedrooms and cleaning bathrooms. Downstairs the washing machine hummed, and Mirry's dress, carefully handwashed, was outside drying off, ready for ironing later in the day.

The telephone rang while she was preparing a casserole of veal for the evening meal.

'Well, Bea, I believe you've got the job,' announced Peter Staines.

'Yes, I start next Monday.' She frowned as she remembered the distinctly challenging way in which Benedict had made his announcement about her job to Elliott this morning. It had almost been as though ... as though he had expected Elliott to forbid her to take it, Beatrice realised on a sudden spurt of resentment. As though Elliott Chalmers had any jurisdiction over her. But why should Benedict do that?

Before she could puzzle any further, Peter was continuing firmly, 'Now, Bea, you mustn't let that family of yours persuade you out of taking this job. It will be good for you, and besides, you've got a perfectly adequate housekeeper who...'

'Had,' Beatrice interrupted him him wryly. 'Mrs Meadows has left.' There was a brief silence from the other end of the line. 'Don't worry, though, Uncle Peter. I'm still taking the job.'

She hadn't realised until that moment just how determined to do so she was. Especially if by so doing she was in some way going against Elliott, she acknowledged, although what possible difference it could make to him whether she worked or not she did not know.

They chatted on for a while about Jon Sharman's musical talent until Peter announced that he had an appointment and rang off.

The afternoons were normally the only time of day Beatrice could call her own, but today, because of Mrs Meadows's defection, she had to drive to their nearest supermarket and stock up on food. When she came back she felt drained and tired, and there was still the rest of the housework to tackle, she remembered as she unlocked the front door. She was dreading ringing the agency and reporting yet another failure.

The telephone rang just as she finished putting away her shopping. She picked it up wearily, tensing as she heard Elliott's clipped tones.

'Are you due out anywhere this afternoon?' he demanded crisply.

'No.' Cursing herself for telling him the truth, she asked warily, 'Why?'

'I've arranged for someone to come round. She used to be my nanny before your mother married my father. She's been living in semi-retirement for some time, but she's agreed to see you.'

'*She's* agreed to come round and see *me*?' Beatrice was both ragingly angry and baffled. How dare Elliott make these sort of high-handed arrangements without discussing them with her first! What was he playing at?

'Thank you, Elliott,' she responded with a crispness that nearly rivalled his own, 'but unfortunately I have no need of a nanny right now!'

'Unfortunately?' She heard him chuckle. 'If that's really what you think, the situation could soon be remedied, Bea.'

The laughter threading through the words, the picture immediately conjured up by his mocking comment momentarily stunned her as she fought against the refined cruelty of his words. Surely a man like Elliott, a connoisseur of women if all she heard about him was true, must see how remote was the possibility of her ever having her own child or children. He might not know in all its detail the paucity of her love life, but she suspected he had a pretty good idea. She might not actually be the only twenty-seven-year-old virgin in the western hemisphere, but there were times when it felt suspiciously like it.

And it wasn't even by choice, she thought indignantly. She'd like to have seen him trying to conduct a passionate affair surrounded by four inquisitive and highly interested younger siblings!

'Come on, Bea, the thought of being a mother can't be that shocking, although to be honest with you that wasn't exactly what I had in mind.'

No, she could just imagine it wasn't, Beatrice thought bitterly.

'Then perhaps you'd be kind enough to explain exactly why this…this person is coming to see me,' she demanded in frigid accents.

He laughed again, the disembodied sound making her shiver disturbingly.

'Now, Bea,' he chided, 'don't go all Sarah Siddons on me, it doesn't suit you. I approached Henrietta to see if she'd be prepared to take over the post vacated by Mrs Meadows.'

'Thank you, Elliott,' Beatrice responded again with awful calm, once she had recovered from her shock, 'but I think I'm perfectly capable of finding my own housekeeper.'

'Oh, any number of them,' Elliott agreed affably. 'But finding them isn't the problem, is it? And besides,' he continued after allowing a telling pause for his comment to sink in, 'I don't think it's a housekeeper so much that you need. Someone more along the lines of a warden from one of Her Majesty's prisons would be more like it,' he continued reflectively, 'or perhaps an ex-public-school matron...'

As she slammed the phone down on him, she was sure she could hear him laughing.

Odious...horrible...detestable, interfering man! she raged, scrubbing the kitchen table with a sudden upsurge of vigour; and if he thought for one moment that she would seriously entertain employing his ex-nanny...

An hour later, feeling rather bemused, Beatrice had the suspicion that the boot was rather on the other foot.

Henrietta, as her visitor firmly informed her she wished to be addressed, appeared to be a martinet of the old school, who, as she told a dazed Beatrice, was very particular about those for whom she worked.

'Of course, when Master Elliott asked me to consider coming to work for you...' She paused, but the expression on her face was a revelation to

Beatrice. 'Such a delightful little boy he was! But you have rather a large household here,' she continued briskly.

'Yes . . . but . . . Well, what we need is a housekeeper rather than a nanny,' Beatrice told her as gently as she could. Against her will she had found herself drawn to this small upright woman with her plain face and forthright views.

'Oh yes, I know that, but when I was first a nursery maid they taught us properly, housework included, although I'm only a plain cook. To be honest with you, looking after small children is too much for me these days; I get a touch of rheumatism in the winter and I can't run after them the way I once could.

'Three brothers and a sister you've got, so Master Elliott said . . .'

Her decision had nothing to do with Elliott at all, Beatrice told herself defensively later; it was the appeal in those words, the faint wistfulness in the other woman's smile, and her own imagination as she compared the empty lonely life that had unwittingly been described to her with the hustle and bustle of her own.

It was perhaps just as well that she didn't see the light in her new employee's eyes as she walked briskly down the road.

If there was one thing she liked, Henrietta Parker reflected happily as she went home, it was a challenge. That dear boy Elliott had been quite right. She was far too young and active to retire. The Bellaire clan was exactly what she needed.

Totally unaware of what she was unleashing on her family, Beatrice started her preparations for their supper.

Mirry's dress, washed and ironed, hung upstairs in her room. All the bathrooms had been cleaned and supplied with fresh towels. The discarded clothes she had found in every room but Elliott's had been washed and put back in their rightful places.

She had noticed that Lucilla's clothes were still in her room, so presumably she had not yet made up her mind about leaving. If Elliott must meddle in their affairs, why couldn't he confine his meddling to where it was most needed? Beatrice thought waspishly. In other words, why couldn't he confine it to his own half-sister?

Mirry was the first to arrive home, lifting an eyebrow when she saw her elder sister's untidy state.

'You're going to have to get your skates on if you're going to be ready for Elliott.'

Turning away so that Mirry wouldn't see the slow burn of anger reddening her skin, Beatrice said as calmly as she could, 'Oh, that's all off now.'

'I suppose he only wanted to talk to you about paying you rent or some such thing while he's living here. On the way to town this morning he asked me how much we pay,' she added, munching an apple she had picked out of the fruit bowl, her eyebrows lifting expressively. 'Honestly, as if we pay anything!'

Beatrice refrained from pointing out that although she only had her grant both Benedict and Sebastian were now earning reasonable amounts of money, certainly enough to buy themselves new and definitely sporty-looking cars, and in Benedict's case a wardrobe full of new clothes.

Was that why Elliott wanted to take her out? Until that moment she had not got round to thinking much about any possible motive, being too incensed over his high-handed announcement of his intention.

That being the case, and knowing that the last thing she wanted to do was to spend an evening with him, she couldn't understand the small stab of disappointment deep inside her.

She was still in the kitchen preparing vegetables for the evening meal when Elliott came in.

'Well, Cinders, not ready yet?' he commented as he walked into the kitchen and put down his briefcase.

As always whenever she was with him Beatrice immediately became aware of a prickly defensiveness coupled with an intense awareness of him.

'I'm not going out with you, Elliott,' she told him angrily.

'Oh yes, you are.' She could see him looking at her stubborn closed face, and her working clothes.

'You know,' he said softly, 'I'm quite prepared to take you dressed like that. It won't be quite what the other female guests are wearing, but if you're not worried about that, then I'm certainly not. You'll definitely stand out—but then isn't that what a Bellaire likes?'

Too many thoughts crowded into her brain at once, and she could only stare furiously at him.

'Temper, temper!' he chided her gently, tapping her cheek with one long forefinger, and then casually picking up a piece of carrot and chewing it.

Anger exploded inside her, filling her with heat, enveloping her like a dark red mist, the force of it making her tremble.

'I am *not* going out with you, Elliott.'

'Oh yes, you are.' All at once his easy calmness dropped away, revealing a grim determination powerful enough to alarm her. He placed his hands either side of her on the table, imprisoning her against him, standing so close to her that she could almost feel his body heat. 'You're coming out with me tonight, whatever it takes to get you there, and that includes taking you upstairs and physically stripping and re-dressing you myself. *I* might enjoy that experience, but I doubt that you would. How many men have seen you naked, Beatrice?' he demanded softly, watching the betraying tremble of her mouth with pitiless eyes.

What was more frightening than his threat was the ease with which her brain conjured up a mental picture of what he had threatened. She trembled, her eyes darkening in a bewilderment that he registered as she sought to suppress the shockingly intimate picture of herself like that in his arms . . .

'I . . .'

'What's the matter?' he goaded softly. 'Does the thought of being with a man frighten you so much that it renders you speechless? Or is it the fact that it's never happened at all?' he probed cruelly.

All at once her control broke. 'Stop it!' she moaned frantically, covering her face with her hands. 'I . . .'

'I mean what I'm saying, Beatrice,' he told her warningly. 'Either you go upstairs now and get ready to come out with me, or I do it for you.'

She let her hands drop and looked into his eyes and knew that he meant every single word he said.

As he stepped away from her she felt so shaky that she could barely stand up. She had to do what he said; she had no alternative. Her bruised mind had trouble in accepting the awful reality of it.

Somehow she made it to her room. She was standing in front of her wardrobe, surveying its contents in dazed shock, when the door opened.

For a moment she thought it was Elliott come to enforce his threat and she froze, but when she turned round she saw that it was only Mirry, who now stood just inside the door, surveying her with a frowningly critical intensity.

'Elliott sent me up to help you find something to wear.'

Almost defensively Beatrice was already reaching for her black velvet, but Mirry whipped it from her, frowning horribly.

'No, not that. It makes you look like a middle-aged spinster, if such a thing still exists.'

'But it's all I've got.'

'Mm . . .' Still frowning, Mirry said, 'Hang on, I won't be a minute.'

She was back in less than five carrying a clear perspex box; inside it was something in brilliant jade-green satin.

'I filched this from Lucilla's room. Don't worry,' she chided as she saw Beatrice's worried expression. 'She won't even notice it's gone. It's one of her mistakes, but it'll look great on you. Look...'

Beatrice felt her eyes rounding in appalled despair as Mirry shook out the rich fabric.

It was a blouse, only a blouse like none that she would ever dream of wearing. It had a demure collar and three-quarter dolman sleeves, but its sole fastening was two long ties at the front that apparently knotted in a large bow. Beatrice stared at it with horrified and fascinated eyes, wondering how Mirry ever thought she would be able to wear an article like that that quite plainly needed to be worn without a bra.

'I can't wear that,' she said wildly at last. 'It's...it's... It would be indecent!'

'Rubbish, you'd look stunning in it,' Mirry corrected firmly. 'It looked ridiculous on Lucilla; she's far too flat-chested.'

'I can't wear it. It would mean going without a bra...'

'So?' countered Mirry, eyeing her judiciously. 'Come on, Bea, you've got exactly the right sort of figure for it. Catch me hiding away my main assets, if I had a figure like yours!' she added teasingly, watching the flush of colour come and go in Beatrice's pale face. 'Look, it isn't that shocking once it's on,' she told her, taking pity on her. 'Just try it and see.'

'I haven't got anything I could wear with it.' For which she was eternally grateful, Beatrice thought fervently, recognising the light of determination in her sister's eyes.

'Of course you have,' said Mirry. 'There's that black silk skirt.'

Beatrice frowned and then remembered. The skirt belonged to a two-piece she had bought on impulse in the sales, and then discarded, feeling that the vivid cerise and black top really did nothing for her.

The skirt in question was short and fitted her perfectly... too perfectly, she thought despairingly now, knowing that once Mirry got the bit between her teeth, so to speak, she would not let go. One look at her sister's determined, vivid face told her that as far as Mirry was concerned her elder sister's transformation into someone fit to be taken out by a man of Elliott's discrimination was becoming a cross between a challenge and a vocation.

'Trust me,' Mirry pleaded now, confirming her thoughts. 'After all, it is my job, and you can't possibly go out with Elliott wearing that ghastly velvet rag.'

Somehow or other, mainly due to the threat of Elliott being called upstairs to give his view on Mirry's chosen outfit, Beatrice allowed herself to be bullied into 'just trying it on'.

This took some time longer than envisaged, due to the fact that Mirry insisted on running back to her own room to find a pair of sheer black tights, essential with the silk skirt, so she assured Beatrice. Beatrice had never worn black tights in her life; she always stuck to brown.

Rather grudgingly, Mirry agreed that she could wear her faithful black satin pumps, and somehow

Beatrice found that she had allowed herself to be
chivvied into her sister's chosen outfit.

Mirry wouldn't let her look at herself in the mirror until she had everything on. She grinned when
Beatrice rather blushingly agreed to remove her bra.

'Honestly, Bea,' she teased, 'I'm your sister, not
some rampant male intent on having his wicked way
with you! Don't worry so much. It's not as though
Elliott has designs on you either, but we want him
to be proud of you, don't we? You're not doing this
for yourself,' she added with mock gravity. 'Think
instead that you're doing it for the family.' She assumed a soulful expression, and then spoiled the
whole effect by giggling.

'You know, you do have a really sizzling figure.
You shouldn't cover it up so much with those awful
bulky sweatshirts and things.'

She tied the satin blouse in the requisite bow as
she finished speaking and then gently turned Bea to
face the mirror.

'There,' she said softly. 'Now you can look.'

Bea didn't know if she dared, but at last she
plucked up her courage and studied her reflection.

Her legs in their black tights looked unfamiliarly
slender, her ankles almost fragilely narrow. The
skirt, rather too faithfully for her taste, followed the
curvy outline of her hips, narrowing into her waist.
The blouse...She could feel heat scorching her skin
as she saw what the blouse did to her body.

The deeply slashed neckline revealed a long dart
of pale creamy flesh; the satin hinted at rather than
moulded the voluptuous shape of her breasts, but it
was plain for everyone and anyone to see that she

wasn't wearing anything underneath it, Beatrice thought frantically, and she was just starting to pluck at the bow, desperate to take it off, when Elliott rapped on her door and walked in.

Mirry greeted him with relief.

'Elliott, doesn't Bea look great? She thinks everyone's going to be staring at her because she isn't wearing a . . .'

'Mirry, please!' begged Beatrice in agonised accents. She knew that her face was bright red and there was no way she could look at Elliott. She waited in mute agony for him to make some sardonic comment, but to her relief all he said was, 'You look fine, Beatrice. I'm afraid there isn't time for you to change again—I promised my friends we'd be there at eight.'

He had barely looked at her, Beatrice realised on a surge of relief as he left the room; hadn't exhibited the slightest bit of notice in her or her body. It was disconcerting that relief should mingle so oddly with pique.

'There you are,' Mirry told her triumphantly. 'You look fine. Now just let me put a bit of make-up on for you and do your hair.'

It was useless to protest, Mirry was well into her stride. She supposed she ought to be relieved that she didn't want to paint her skin with colourful butterflies like her own, Beatrice reflected wryly as she surveyed the undoubtedly flattering addition of soft jade eyeshadow and warm pink lip gloss to her suddenly luminescent face.

'I don't know why you always wear your hair up,' Mirry complained as she unpinned and brushed it.

'It's got a lovely natural curl.' Like a magician she produced a couple of tortoiseshell combs, deftly clipping back the soft auburn hair and somehow achieving a style that was both attractive and chic.

'Now remember, no coming in late.' Mirry grinned, wagging a forefinger at her. 'And no letting Elliott run out of petrol on the way back!' Her teasing laughter followed Beatrice downstairs.

As though by magic, Elliott appeared in the hall just as she came downstairs, and somehow managed to whisk her outside and into his car before she could protest that she hadn't said goodbye to the boys.

At the back of her mind had been the conviction that somehow either Benedict or William would need something doing that would legitimately prevent her from accompanying Elliott, but now it was too late; he was setting the car in motion and they were on their way.

But to where, she wondered with a start, and with whom? He had told her nothing about his plans for the evening or his purpose in forcing her to accompany him.

CHAPTER THREE

BEATRICE had got into Elliott's car determined to express her dislike of the way he had outmanoeuvred her by not voluntarily addressing so much as a single word to him, but she soon discovered her guns were well and truly spiked when Elliott turned on the tape machine and, far from appearing to want to engage her in conversation, seemed perfectly content to listen to the Bach pouring smoothly from his car's powerful speakers.

There is nothing, Beatrice decided wrathfully, quite as infuriating as a person who refuses to give one the opening for a justifiable venting of one's temper. They had only gone a hundred yards or so when she became aware that she had made a grave tactical error, and she suspected from the grin that flashed across Elliott's face as he surveyed her stormy countenance that he was well aware of the state of her temper.

They appeared to be driving towards Chelsea, but although she was aching to ask him where they were going she forced herself to keep silent.

When he parked his car in an attractive Chelsea mews, she deliberately averted her head. She heard him laugh softly beside her, and she could almost feel the tiny hairs lifting on her skin as she fought to subdue her fury.

As they climbed the small flight of steps outside one of the mews houses, Elliott relented and leaned towards her, so close that she could feel the warmth of his breath against her ear in a distinctly disturbing fashion.

'Some friends of mine are having a housewarming. I think you'll like them.'

'Not if they're friends of yours I won't,' Beatrice muttered bitterly beneath her breath.

She saw his eyebrows lift, but before he could say anything the front door was opened and a tiny blonde was flinging herself recklessly into Elliott's arms.

'Elliott darling, you made it after all!'

It was several seconds before he was released, seconds during which Beatrice stood icily to one side, wondering bitterly why on earth he had insisted on dragging her out with him.

'Shelley, this is Beatrice,' Elliott introduced when the blonde had released him.

The speculative look to which she was subjected told Beatrice that Shelley was not predisposed to approve of her. The blonde was not only tiny, but so slim that she made Beatrice feel positively clumsy.

'David and the others are in the drawing-room,' she said at last, her smile warning Beatrice that she was reserving judgement on her. 'Go through and help yourself to drinks!'

Beatrice didn't recognise any faces among the crowd of people milling round the attractive drawing-room, but then she hadn't expected to. Elliott moved in a different milieu from the stage and television world her parents and the rest of her family inhabited, and although he was scrupulous about introducing her, she was too conscious of the covert interest the two of them were causing to concentrate on the other guests' names.

She was longing to ask why Elliott had insisted on her accompanying him, and now bitterly regretted her silence in the car. She suspected from the mocking smile that Elliott gave her that he was perfectly aware of her feelings, and that, infuriatingly, he was amused by them.

The party was a very relaxed affair, and if she hadn't been so angry with Elliott she suspected she might have enjoyed it. Rather guiltily she discovered that it was a relief to be in the company of people whose interests did not lie exclusively in the world of drama. It was also a relief not to be constantly on the receiving end of comments and questions about her illustrious parents and the inevitable and unflattering comparisons that went with them.

In fact if she was honest she was enjoying herself far more than she had done in ages, and it was rather an unpleasant shock to be interrupted by Elliott just as she was settling comfortably into an interesting discussion on the merits and demerits of Nouvelle Cuisine with a fellow guest.

'Sorry, James, but I'm afraid I'm going to have to take her away from you,' Elliott drawled lightly, coming up behind her and placing his arm round her shoulders.

Beatrice was stunned to see her companion flush slightly before excusing himself and hurrying off. Correctly interpreting her puzzled frown, Elliott murmured against her ear, 'He's frightened he might have been poaching.'

His arm was still around her and, quite inexplicably, as she started to move away it tightened, imprisoning her against his side.

Wary of an undignified struggle, and knowing that Elliott was delighting in tormenting her, Beatrice demanded crossly, 'Why on earth should he think that . . .'

' . . . you and I are lovers?' Elliott asked softly.

Beatrice could feel the hot colour sweeping over her skin. It was ridiculous to react to his provocation in so gauche a manner, but she couldn't help it. Elliott knew quite well that she hadn't been about to say anything like that at all, and as she fought to get her embarrassment under control, she was amazed to discover that mingled with her anger was a fine thread of pain that came from the realisation that a man like Elliott could never desire a woman as ordinary as her.

'Tell me a bit more about this job you've got.'

The resentment she would normally have felt at his inquisitiveness was lost beneath the relief of finding herself on more familiar and firmer ground. As calmly as she could, she told him about her new job.

'You mean you're giving up nursemaiding your family to take on nursemaiding *one* man instead,' he mocked when she had finished.

His comment hurt, not just because of its kernel of truth but because it underlined the fact that she had neither the qualifications nor the training to equip her for anything else.

She was glad that their hostess chose that moment to interrupt them. The diminutive blonde was obviously one of Elliott's fans, Beatrice decided waspishly. Maybe at one time before her marriage they could even have been lovers.

It worried her, this uncomfortable awareness she seemed to have developed of Elliott as a man. Hitherto all her awareness of him had concentrated on the antipathy she felt towards him, and her awareness of his own indulgent contempt towards her family. She realised with a small sense of shock that beneath her dislike there was also a faint thread of fear. But fear of what? How on earth could *Elliott* possibly threaten her? Their lives barely impinged on one another.

But they were doing, now that they were sharing the same roof.

Several times tonight he had introduced her as his new 'landlady' and she had been furiously aware of the interpretation some of her fellow guests had put on that description. It had been quite obvious that they thought that she and Elliott were lovers and that he had moved in with her, but she was all too miserably conscious of how ridiculous she would sound if she tackled Elliott on the subject. He would probably tell her she was imagining things, she decided bitterly; indeed, he might even take it into that Machiavellian mind of his to suggest that she was not just indulging in imagination but in wishing it were true as well.

It was gone midnight when he skilfully disengaged her from the group she was talking with, his hand oh, so casually tucking her against his side in a manner that made several of their fellow guests eye them knowingly. And yet there was nothing particularly proprietorial in his touch, so how could she complain?

'Come on, Cinders,' he drawled lightly. 'It's way past your bedtime.'

Infuriatingly Beatrice felt herself flush betrayingly—not because their fellow guests were so obviously thinking that he wanted to take her home to make love to her—how could it be that, when she herself knew he had no desire to do so?—but because of that mocking reminder of his earlier taunt in calling her 'Cinders'.

She hadn't been gifted with the silvered tongue of the rest of her family, and she knew it was useless to risk indulging in verbal swordplay with Elliott anyway. She had heard him too often both with Lucilla and Benedict. Beneath that solid, powerfully muscled body lurked a subtle and dangerous psyche far too complex and deadly for her to master.

'Enjoy yourself?' Elliott asked her as he opened the car door for her.

She was just about to let him know exactly what she thought of the way he had compelled her to accompany him, when the moon edged out behind a cloud and she caught the anticipatory and mocking gleam in his eyes.

'Why is it you're so determined to provoke me?' she sighed instead. 'You force me to come with you ... You ...'

'I what?' he invited, helpfully waiting until she had fastened her seatbelt before he started the engine.

'It's almost as though you actually want me to lose my temper,' Beatrice told him, perplexed.

He laughed softly and mocked, 'Got it in one, Bella Beatrice.'

His laughter and the cruelty of that oh, so inappropriate nickname made her instinctively withdraw into herself. She knew she wasn't beautiful; there was no need for Elliott to underline the fact.

She had taught herself to accept that the unthinking and sometimes unkind comments of her family sprang from their own lack of awareness of how much they could hurt, but where Elliott was concerned she was prepared to make no such allowances. He knew exactly what he was doing.

She ignored his comment and averted her head to stare out of her window, and when eventually she did glance at him again, he was concentrating on the road with a rather grim smile.

She hadn't realised how tense she was until they turned into the familiar drive and Elliott stopped the car. When she breathed out, even her ribs seemed to ache as though her whole body had been under intense pressure.

As she turned to open her door, she realised that it was locked, and automatically she looked back at Elliott. He had moved in his seat so that he was facing her, his expression hidden from her by the shadows. She opened her mouth to ask him to unlock the door, but he forestalled her, questioning lazily, 'Why did you get so uptight and embarrassed when Mirry mentioned the fact that you aren't wearing a bra?'

Her fingers curled tightly into the palms of her hands as she fought the hideous wave of shamed embarrassment engulfing her.

He let her wait several seconds before adding, 'Why are you so uncomfortable about your body, Beatrice? It it because it isn't the Bellaire body? Because you aren't tall and flat-chested like the rest of the clan?'

She couldn't take in the fact that she was actually sitting with him and listening to this. It was so out of character, so alien to everything that had gone before. She had always suspected that Elliott didn't particularly like her, but hitherto his dislike had always taken the form of the same amused contempt he showed all the rest of her family. Never once before had he singled her out the way he was doing now. Never before . . .

As her senses relayed to her the fact that inexplicably the distance between them seemed to have narrowed considerably, she struggled to respond to his comments in a suitably cutting fashion, but could only manage a confused mingling of, 'I . . . They . . . You . . .'

'Yes?' Elliott encouraged helpfully. 'You . . . They . . . I . . . What? Is it this, Bea?' he demanded, his voice suddenly roughly unfamiliar, one hand imprisoning her waist while the other smoothed up over her ribcage, pausing to measure the frantic thud of her heart before gently cupping the full swell of her breast.

A confusion of sensations jammed her thoughts: shock widened her eyes, tension locked her throat, panic and shame blurring her eyes as she felt the traitorous response of her flesh to that too-knowing male touch, and realised how easily Elliott's hand cupped the fullness of her breast.

As if the shock of all that wasn't enough, his thumb stroked softly over the satin just where it rested against her nipple. She wasn't so naïve that she knew nothing about the workings of the human body, but that her own body should respond so vibrantly and instantly was shaming in the extreme, and with a kind of sick fascination she watched as the subtle caress of Elliott's thumb caused her nipple to push provocatively against the jade satin as if it actively sought the continuation of his tormenting stimulation.

Hazel eyes blind with shock and shame, Beatrice trembled visibly.

Elliott's head blotted out the light, mercifully concealing her own body from her sight, his mouth against her ear as he whispered laconically, 'Why so shocked? You must have experienced this before—and enjoyed it. Or is it because the giver of the pleasure is me? Well, I'll tell you something that will shock you even more.' His voice seemed to have hardened, a peculiar tension emanating from his body that even in her stunned state she registered. 'I'm enjoying it too. So much so that . . .' His voice became muffled and distant as he pushed her back against her seat, his fingers easing the satin fabric aside so that his mouth could caress the bared flesh of her breast.

She shuddered, unable to control that small betraying spasm of mingled shock and pleasure.

Against her will, she felt her spine arch. A small sob of horror locked in her throat as she raised her hands to push him away and found her wrists gripped in powerful fingers that forced her arms to drop impotently away while his mouth continued to explore the soft swell of her breast, all the time edging closer and closer to the betraying thrust of her nipple.

The moon emerged from behind a cloud, illuminating the inside of the car as Beatrice looked helplessly down on Elliott's sleek dark head.

Although he was using his superior strength to prevent her from pushing him away, the soul-deep honesty she possessed, which had never been part of the Bellaire personality, forced her to admit that there was a mindless, almost savage pleasure to be found in his deliberate ravishment of her senses; a dangerous and frightening urge to respond recklessly to her female conditioning that ached to be free to respond to the deliberate incitement of his mouth.

She had to fight hard to remember that this was Elliott caressing her, Elliott who never did anything without a subtle purpose, but she resisted the shaming desire to arch eagerly against the mind-destroying pleasure offered by his mouth and instead remained stoically unmoving as his mouth moved delicately towards its goal.

For the first time in her life she knew what it meant actually to feel a silence. The atmosphere inside the car was such that she hardly dared to breathe lest she betrayed herself, but when Elliott's mouth found the goal it sought and closed over it with a thick sound of satisfaction she was powerless to stop the surge of sensation shooting through her.

Elliott had released her arms, but she was powerless to lift them to push him away. It took every ounce of concentration she had to suppress the shudders of pleasure pulsing through her as his hands smoothed aside the satin of her blouse to completely expose her breasts.

Even so, Elliott was the one who heard the car coming down the drive and reacted to it, drawing away from her and covering her with her blouse in one swift movement, but when she turned in panic for the car door he stopped her, shaking his head and saying quietly, 'Wait a few minutes. You can't go in yet.'

She was just about to object when she glanced down and saw the shaming evidence of the pleasure he had given her straining against the fabric of her shirt. Her whole body went hot with embarrassment, and as Elliott reached towards her, she pulled away tensely.

She was desperate to get away from him. Her whole body felt scorched with shame and humiliation. She wasn't sure what he had been trying to prove in making her respond to him like that. She was just about to demand that he let her out of the car, when Lucilla knocked on the passenger window.

Elliott released the electronic mechanism, opening it.

'What are you two doing sitting out here?' She glared malevolently at Beatrice.

'We were just chatting.'

'Poor Elliott, you must be really enjoying being a martyr,' Lucilla commented acidly.

Beatrice swallowed the hard lump that seemed to be stuck in her throat. She didn't need Lucilla to underline her shortcomings for her.

She wasn't going to demean herself by demanding an explanation from Elliott, she decided tiredly. That was probably just what he wanted her to do. Elliott enjoyed playing cat-and-mouse games, only this time the mouse wasn't going to play. Oh, no doubt he had enjoyed her naïveté and her embarrassment, and no doubt he would have equally enjoyed baiting her while she tried to find an explanation for his extraordinary behaviour, but she wasn't going to give him the opportunity to do so.

When he opened the window Elliott had released the door lock, and now she opened the door and got out, saying as calmly as she could, 'I really must go in. I don't want to oversleep again tomorrow.'

Remarkably she managed to make it to her room without being intercepted by anyone.

Loud pop music thundered out of Mirry's room, and since neither of the twins' cars had been outside she assumed they must still be out. William would be asleep. She counted herself fortunate that none of her too-sharp-eyed family had witnessed her return.

Only when she was protectively wrapped in her cotton nightdress and huddled beneath the bedcovers did Beatrice judge it safe to allow herself to think about those bewildering moments in Elliott's car.

How he would laugh at her if he knew that his had been the first male lips to caress her so intimately, and no doubt he would be even more amused to know that she was still affected by the memory of his touch.

She had no idea what deep game he was playing with her, but one thing she did know was that she would be wise to give him as little opportunity to indulge in it as possible.

CHAPTER FOUR

IT was a decision Beatrice kept very much to the forefront of her mind for the next couple of days, carefully juggling her schedules so that she came into as little contact with Elliott as possible.

A letter arrived on Thursday morning addressed to her which momentarily banished Elliott from her thoughts. She opened it after breakfast, and gnawed uncertainly at her bottom lip as she studied its contents.

She would, so Henrietta Parker informed her, be arriving to take up her new position with the family on Saturday morning.

As yet Beatrice had not broken the news to her siblings that she, or rather Elliott, had found them a new housekeeper, and she suspected from various comments that had been dropped since Mrs Meadows's abdication that the news would not be well received.

William had confided artlessly only the previous teatime that he much preferred her cooking to Mrs Meadows's, and Benedict had told her winningly over breakfast one morning that no one could iron his cotton shirts as well as she could.

Out of the corner of her eye Beatrice had seen the pages of Elliott's *Financial Times* flicker slightly, but he had made no comment other than to offer drily, 'You should try Jeeves laundry service, Benedict. I find them excellent, although of course *their* services don't come free.'

There had been a distinct glint of temper in Benedict's eyes, she remembered now.

Even without her own ambivalent feelings towards him, having Elliott in the house was not easy. She winced sometimes when she overheard the sardonic taunts Benedict made to him, but when she had hesitantly suggested to her brother that he might be carrying things rather too far he had shrugged and said lazily, 'Oh, Elliott's far too stoical to rise to any bait I might dangle.'

Exasperated as much by Benedict's inability to understand that *she* might not care for the almost constant atmosphere in the house as by her fear that Elliott was simply biding his time, she responded rather waspishly that she thought he would have had better things to do with his time.

'Getting to you, is he, Bea?' he remarked. 'Don't worry, he won't be here much longer. What did he want the other night when he took you out?' he asked casually.

Beatrice froze. This was the first time any member of her family had commented on her date with Elliott, and she literally didn't know what to say.

She was saved, albeit unknowingly, by Mirry, who wandered into the kitchen just in time to catch Benedict's question.

'Oh, he just wanted to talk to you about what rent he should pay while he's staying here, didn't he, Bea?' she answered for her.

She knew she was flushing, all too conscious from Benedict's narrow-eyed scrutiny that he suspected she was concealing something from him. Sometimes, when he looked at her like that, there was almost something calculating in his expression, and yet Benedict was the least calculating person she knew. Of course he was very protective towards her...too protective sometimes. Guiltily she smothered the thought.

'You know, Bea, I can't understand why he isn't staying at a hotel. Surely he'd be much more comfortable than living here? And it isn't as though he's short of money. He could easily afford it.'

'Oh, I think Lucilla offered, and I suppose he didn't want to offend her by refusing.'

Benedict's eyebrows rose as he snorted in derision. 'Come on, Bea! This is *Elliott* we're talking about. Since when has he ever cared about treading on anyone's toes?'

For a moment resentment flashed in the brilliant blue eyes, and Beatrice remembered that when he was nineteen Benedict had approached Elliott for a loan to help him buy a fast sports car he coveted. She had felt only relief when Elliott had refused in no uncertain terms, but she realised for the first time that perhaps that refusal still rankled.

Benedict was not as mature as he liked to think, she decided indulgently. Elliott had acted only in his best interests, able to see, as Benedict apparently still could not, the potential hazard of a powerful car in the hands of a young and unskilled driver.

'I like having him here,' Mirry interjected.

'Because he gives you a lift to work? Or are you hoping for something more from him than simply a free ride, little sister? If so, be warned, he's way out of your class.'

The dark head tossed as Mirry showed her contempt of such elder-brotherly concern.

'I know that. Besides, he's miles too old for me. Anyway, he's better suited to Bea.' She grinned at her sister's shocked expression and said enigmatically, 'I think you've met your match, brother dear.'

Beatrice tensed as she saw the thunderclouds gather in Benedict's eyes. Of all of them he was the one who had inherited the greatest degree of temperament. He could change from sunny smiles to thunder frowns all within the space of a few seconds. Unlike the stoical William and the less aggressive Sebastian, he was the one who had clung the hardest after their parents' death.

'Don't take on this new job, Bea,' he said abruptly now. 'We need you here, at home, especially now that we've lost Mrs Meadows.'

Here was her cue, but even so she almost missed it, leaping into a disorganised flutter of words that made Benedict frown and glower at her.

'What do you mean—another housekeeper?'

'I was going to tell you all about it tonight,' she apologised. 'I only had her letter of acceptance this morning. I wasn't sure that she'd want to take the job, even though Elliott . . .'

'Elliott?'

'Well, she was his nanny,' Beatrice told him, 'and when Elliott realised that Mrs Meadows had left he suggested she might be prepared to step into her shoes.'

She could tell that Benedict was furious, and she could feel herself tensing in anticipation of a scene. What was it about her that made her so unlike the rest of her family? Where they relished high drama, she dreaded it. All of them apart from her would throw themselves into an argument with careless disregard for its consequences, while all she could do was close her ears and pray that it would soon be over.

'A nanny?' Benedict now said bitterly. 'Well, thanks very much, Bea! We aren't children, you know.'

'No? Well, try proving it, and accept that your sister has a right to live her own life, just as much as the rest of you do.'

The cool intercession of Elliott's voice, just when she was least expecting it, caused Beatrice to tremble violently. She could tell that Benedict was furiously angry, but instead of retaliating as she had expected, he stormed out of the kitchen, slamming the door violently behind him.

'Definitely a case of spare the rod and spoil the child,' Elliott remarked *sotto voce* as Benedict left. 'I take it you've decided to employ Henrietta, then?'

'I think it was more a case of her deciding to work for us,' Beatrice told him stiffly, turning to face the sink and busying herself wiping the already clean surfaces. If only he could go away; she felt so dreadfully ill at ease, so humiliatingly aware of what had happened in his car. She could feel her skin burning with embarrassed heat and prayed desperately for someone to walk into the kitchen.

He came to stand behind her and she felt the tiny hairs at the back of her nape lift in atavistic apprehension.

'Beatrice, I want to talk to you.' His fingers circled her wrist, tugging her round so that she had to face him.

If he said one word about the other night, she would be sick on the spot, she thought frantically with one half of her brain, while the other acknowledged that she had always known this moment would come, when he would exact the full measure of enjoyment from her humiliation and shame.

'Come and sit down.'

She let him lead her over to the table, and sank down into the chair he pulled out for her.

What was he going to do? Taunt her for her betraying response to him? Tell her why he had done it, why he had so deliberately and effectively aroused her? Numbly she sat there waiting for the blow to fall.

'I want to talk to you about Lucilla.'

The shock of his totally unexpected words made her lift her head and stare at him.

'Lucilla?' She said her half-sister's name as though it was totally foreign to her.

'Yes, you know, Lucilla, our mutual half-sister...and mutual cross,' he added with a trace of sardonic amusement. 'I take it she's still seeing this producer she's so keen on?'

He wanted to talk to her about Lucilla. Beatrice could barely take it in, her brain struggling to accommodate this new information, and the oddly let-down feeling that accompanied it.

'Yes... at least, I think she is,' she agreed, her mind on automatic pilot. 'But it's no good asking me to speak to her, Elliott. She dislikes me as it is, and...'

'I'm not one of your brothers, Beatrice,' he responded rather grimly, 'and I'm perfectly capable of doing my own dirty work, thank you very much. If there's anything to be said to Lucilla, I suspect I'm far more capable of saying it effectively than you. No, what I want from you is your estimation of just how deeply she's involved with this man.'

As she struggled for self-control, Beatrice wondered wildly if she had strayed into some sort of impossible dream. It was almost as though Elliott was as determined to ignore what had happened between them as she was herself. But why?

She forced herself to switch her attention from her own problems to those of her half-sister.

'Well, they're...'

'Lovers?' Elliott supplied sardonically for her. 'I know that. I'm not interested in the degree of her physical commitment to him, only her emotional vulnerability.' He saw her expression and said sardonically, 'You're wrong, you know. Lucilla is capable of being hurt. Oh, I know she hides it well.'

'She won't listen to anything I might say to her. She... she resents me.'

'Because you're a full Bellaire and she isn't. Surely you must have realised that years ago? She's always been jealous of you, Beatrice.'

Lucilla jealous of her? Beatrice opened her mouth to deny it, and then suddenly, perceiving the truth of Elliott's remark, fell silent.

'You see? You know it's true, even if you've always preferred not to admit it. Lucilla suffers from being neither a true Bellaire nor a true Chalmers—at least in her own eyes. She's just as much a victim of the Bellaire mystique as you are yourself, you know, Bea.' He gave her a few seconds for his remark to sink in and then continued calmly, 'Now, I suspect we're both in agreement that she has to be detached from her blood-sucking friend, but how?'

'You're the one who seems to have all the answers,' she told him rather bitterly.

'Mmm... I thank you for that vote of confidence, but in this case, at least, I suspect it's misplaced. How much do you know about the terms of my father's will?'

Beatrice stared at him.

'Nothing.'

'Mmm. Well, the money he left in trust under my control for Lucilla becomes hers on her thirtieth birthday, or on her marriage, whichever happens first. Horrocks is notoriously short of money. He wants to start up his own production company...'

'And you think he might marry Lucilla...'

'To get his hands on her money. Well, it's certainly a possibility, isn't it? And Lucilla is just about dense enough to go along with him. Only if she does, I suspect she's going to wake up to reality with a hard bump. Horrocks has had a mistress for years—the wife of a prominent politician who doesn't intend to break up her marriage. It's a relationship that appears to suit them both, but it won't, I suspect, suit Lucilla.'

'Have you told her any of this?'

'Not yet. She's not too pleased with me at the moment. I'm afraid I made a foolish mistake—I let her see that I wasn't too happy about the relationship.'

'I don't see what I can do. She won't listen to anything I say.'

'I don't want you to *say* anything. I've managed to find out that Horrocks and his woman friend have dinner once a fortnight at a very small and discreet restaurant in Knightsbridge. If Lucilla could see them there together, I think that might do the trick.' He gave her an oblique smile. 'It's my birthday next week, and I think it might be a rather nice idea if I took my half-sister and her family out to dinner to celebrate the occasion, and that's where I shall need your help.'

'To do what?' Beatrice asked, baffled.

'To muster the full Bellaire clan,' Elliott told her drily. 'Lucilla would think it distinctly odd if I took her out to dinner on our own, but a family birthday celebration . . .'

Beatrice could follow his logic, but it made her feel uneasy; so much could go wrong . . .

'But it's so . . . so underhand,' she protested feebly.

She didn't like the smile Elliott gave her.

'Maybe, but drastic situations call for drastic measures. Perhaps if Benedict was as protective towards Lucilla as he is of you, they wouldn't be necessary, would they?'

There was just enough truth in the criticism to make it sting.

'Oh, but Lucilla isn't . . .'

'What? In need of protection? You're his full sister, and you wonder why she resents you so much!'

'I don't know if I'll be able to persuade the others to go,' she told him, remembering Benedict's earlier anger. 'Ben . . .'

'Oh, they'll go—if you're going,' Elliott responded drily. There was a look in his eyes she couldn't fathom, a knowledge of something outside her own perceptions. It made his mouth twist in wry mockery, and added a hardness to his face that made her shiveringly aware that he could be a very dangerous man.

'You can tell them tonight over dinner—then they'll have two pieces of bad news to chew over together, won't they?' When she looked puzzled, he elucidated mockingly, 'You were going to tell the others tonight that you'd found a substitute for Mrs Meadows, weren't you?'

As luck would have it the whole family were in for supper that evening.

Beatrice raised the subject of Henrietta Parker first. Benedict was still sulking, but refrained from any subversive comment, although there were general moans and groans, until Elliott said pensively, 'Of course you could always share the household chores out between you—then no housekeeper would be needed.'

Absolute silence greeted his remark. The Bellaire family were not used to having the ground cut out from beneath their feet. All of them studied Elliott and then looked at Beatrice.

What did they expect her to do? she wondered half hysterically. Hardening her heart against their united appeal, she said uncomfortably, 'Elliott is quite right. Now that I've taken on this new job I can't manage the house singlehanded.'

'Then give up the job,' Lucilla said sardonically. 'If it's the money angle you're worrying about, I dare say I could scrape around and find something. How much was this composer going to pay you? Not much, I don't suppose.'

An anger the like of which she had never before experienced fired Beatrice's blood. In a voice so quiet that it was almost a whisper, she said slowly, 'Money has nothing to do with it, Lucilla— although I don't suppose you'll be able to understand that, since it seems to rule your world. I'm taking this job because I want to, because . . .'

'Because she simply can't resist going to the rescue of yet another lame dog,' drawled Benedict, interrupting her. Across the table his eyes warned Lucilla that she had gone too far. 'Well, if it means that much to you, Sis, I suppose we'll all just have to endure the ministrations of our new "nanny". Have you warned her about us, Elliott?' he challenged, throwing an acid smile in the direction of the man at the far end of the table.

'Ought I to have done?'

Elliott was calmly buttering a small wholemeal roll, apparently oblivious to the highly contentious undercurrents sizzling round the table.

'Er...all of you, it's Elliott's birthday next week,' Beatrice interrupted nervously, 'and...and...we're all going out to dinner to celebrate the occasion. Next...'

'Tuesday,' Elliott supplied for her.

There was a moment's silence; Beatrice held her breath, already anticipating Benedict's objections, but Mirry spoke first, getting up and flinging her arms theatrically round Elliott's neck.

'Fantastic! Where are you taking us, Elliott? Somewhere really expensive, I hope.'

'It's a surprise,' Elliott responded, adding to Lucilla, 'and it's family only.'

Beatrice bit her lip as she noted her half-sister's rebellious expression. Elliott was manoeuvring them all like a skilled puppetmaster, but would his machinations have the desired effect?

The fact that they had talked together and he had made no mention of her physical response to him had lessened her tension to some degree, although her mind wasn't wholly at rest. Elliott never did anything without a purpose—his actions in regard to Lucilla showed that. There must have been something behind his deliberate arousal of her—and she was quite sure that it *had* been deliberate. At no time had she got the impression that he was a man carried away by a physical desire he could not control.

Perhaps he was just biding his time... Perhaps Lucilla had become more urgently important and so he had been forced to shelve whatever it was he had in mind for her.

It was like having a sword hanging over her head, she acknowledged on Friday evening as she walked in the garden. They had a very large garden, which was kept well tended by the same gardener who had looked after it when her parents first bought the house. He was well into his sixties now, and suffered from rheumatism in the winter. The kitchen garden supplied them with most of their fruit and vegetables. At the end of the summer, Beatrice normally spent the better part of two weeks preserving and bottling fruit, and making jams and chutney.

On Monday she would start her new job... her new life, and she was looking forward to it with a sense of anticipation she had not expected.

Tomorrow Henrietta Parker would arrive, and already she foresaw fireworks, especially from Benedict.

A shadow emerged from the shelter of the fruit trees, startling her. For one desperate moment she thought it was Elliott, her heartbeat only returning to normal when she saw it was Sebastian.

'Do you talk to them?' he teased, indicating the fruit bushes. 'It's supposed to make them give good crops.'

'Of course I don't,' she lied unconvincingly. 'What brings you out here? I thought you had a date tonight.'

'Not until later.' He plucked absently at a bunch of blackcurrents, shredding the fruit and leaves. 'I wanted to have a word with you. Don't pay too much attention to what Ben says. Elliott's right, we *are* a selfish lot, expecting you always to be there, waiting hand and foot on us. It's partially your fault,' he added with a grin. 'You've spoilt us, you know. But don't let Ben's antics stop you from taking this job.'

She was amazingly touched, almost close to tears, and as though he realised it Sebastian added firmly, "And don't let this composer chap get too dependent on you, either. Ben's right about one thing— you are a sucker for lame dogs.'

'Seb...' Something that had been troubling her all week brought a faint frown to her forehead. 'Why is Ben so antagonistic towards Elliott?'

She could sense Sebastian's almost immediate withdrawal, and not for the first time sighed over the intense bond of loyalty that existed between the twins.

'I...I think that's something you should ask him,' he said carefully. 'That is, if you're sure you don't already know.' He saw her bewildered expression and grinned indulgently, ruffling her hair. 'You don't know, do you?' He shook his head ruefully. 'Well, don't worry about it. Ben will get over it. He'll have to—he's no match for Elliott.'

He was gone before Beatrice could query his cryptic remark. Her pleasure in the evening suddenly gone, she made her way back to the house.

Since Elliott had moved in with them they seemed to have suffered an unusual amount of discord. She frowned, wishing the alterations on his flat might suddenly speed forward and remove him from their midst. His presence was too unsettling; it made her too aware of things she would far rather have ignored. It made her aware of herself and her needs as a woman in a way that hurt.

Thinking about him kept her awake at night, her body tense... aching... empty, she admitted guiltily, forced to face the galling knowledge that her body ached for the sensations he had aroused in it, that it ached *for him*!

CHAPTER FIVE

THE dinner party was not going to be a success. Beatrice knew that from the start, but all was not gloom and doom. Amazingly, all her family, but most surprisingly of all, Benedict, had taken to Henrietta Parker's old-fashioned blend of bossiness and spoiling like cats being spoonfed on cream.

Once or twice she had even surprised in herself a brief spasm of jealousy as she saw how quickly her siblings turned from her to Henrietta, as the family had been asked to call their new housekeeper.

Sensibly, Beatrice had told herself that her feelings were quite natural, and had perhaps less sensibly found relief for them in mothering her new employer, who had surrendered himself to this hitherto unexperienced delight in blissful relief.

It took all day Monday for her to restore some sort of order to the small study where she was to work. At lunchtime she had invaded the sanctum of the music room with a bowl of homemade soup and some sandwiches, which she had discreetly left on a tray on the coffee table.

When she went back for the tray an hour later the soup bowl was empty and the sandwiches were gone.

On neither occasion did her employer lift his head from the score he was working on, but without putting it into words both employer and employee felt that an excellent rapport had been struck.

For the first time in a very long time indeed Beatrice returned home to comparative harmony—and to a meal she had not had to prepare herself.

Henrietta told her over supper that she had been through the larder shelves, and was pleased to inform her that she considered this autumn they would make apple and raspberry conserve, and that the blackberries would make into jelly better than they did jam.

Having thus established her superiority, Henrietta went on to assure Beatrice in a kindly voice that she had done very well indeed.

'Very well,' she confirmed, casting an eagle eye round the table and its occupants.

Much to Beatrice's relief, Elliott wasn't there. He was dining with clients, apparently, and Lucilla was also out—no doubt with her producer.

The grins with which her siblings greeted her discomfort did nothing to alleviate Beatrice's feelings, but her moment came when Benedict was chastised for apparently sitting down without washing his hands, and William was told that from now on he would not be allowed to bring books to the table with him.

Amazingly, not one voice was lifted in objection. Beatrice was impressed, despite her own discomfort. She suspected she need not worry about coming home and finding that Henrietta had handed in her notice, and that their new housekeeper was more than a match for any machinations on the part of her family.

Just as she was musing over how unpredictable the human psyche could be in that her family seemed to accept Henrietta's bossiness where it had previously expressed intense outrage at discovering even the faintest suspicion of this trait in previous housekeepers, she remembered how fond her mother had been of a particularly determined and almost shrewish dresser who had once looked after her, and decided that there must be something in the Bellaire personality that enjoyed being bullied— provided that the bullying was done by experts.

She had also noticed that Henrietta was far less inclined to spoil and fuss around her than she did the others, almost as though they were the only two adults amongst a party of feckless children, and she wasn't sure whether she ought to be flattered or up-set.

She certainly found that under the new régime she had far more time for herself. When her friend Annabel telephoned and suggested lunch on the day of Elliott's birthday party, she could not even offer the excuse that she couldn't leave her employer, since Jon was also going out to lunch with his agent. Annabel heartily disapproved of the Bellaire family, and as Beatrice had expected, they had almost reached the end of their main course before she felt she had spent a satisfactory amount of time in verbal condemnation of them.

Several years older than Beatrice, and comfortably married with two children, Annabel was her closest friend—they had met when on the same catering course—and yet, Beatrice realised guiltily as she listened to her, she came nowhere even close to confiding to her what had happened in Elliott's car, and how he had made her feel. She frowned a little over this realisation, surprised to discover how stealthily the habit of standing on her own feet had grown on her. It was of course a legacy of her parents' death coupled with the responsibility for the family. But if she ever needed to do so, who could she lean on? Not Annabel, who made no secret of her disapproval of the rest of the Bellaire clan; not her godfather, who had recently begun to show signs of his age, and who was beginning to look heart-wrenchingly vulnerable.

Unbidden, one face formed a mental picture inside her head; one person who she knew beyond any thought of a doubt had the strength to support any number of clinging vines. But what on earth was she thinking of? Elliott was the very last person she would ever want to cling to, even if she had been the clinging type.

'Beatrice, you aren't listening to a word I'm saying!'

With a shock, Beatrice realised that she had forgotten Annabel completely, so deeply engrossing were her own private thoughts. She apologised, offering the palliative that her new job had been occupying her mind, and was profoundly relieved when Annabel graciously accepted this excuse.

They talked for a while about Beatrice's new job. Annabel had heard of her employer—her husband was an opera buff—and it seemed that Jon Sharman had been invited to join with other up-and-coming young composers in producing a new opera to commemorate the centenary of the company for whom Ian, Annabel's husband, worked.

Annabel grimaced slightly as she delivered this information.

'Hollingbroke's have always had quite a thing about their sponsorship of the arts, and this opera they've commissioned is apparently going to be quite something. They're hoping to put it on at the Opera House. Of course the whole thing is tax deductible, otherwise the accountants would be having forty fits, but I'm beginning to wonder if Ian works for a company that produces consumer durables, or performs operas. The whole company seems to have gone opera-mad!

'By the way,' Annabel added, as she ordered their coffee, 'an old friend asked after you the other day—Tom Leaman.'

Beatrice had been introduced to Tom at one of Annabel's 'duty parties'. They had got on well enough together for her to enjoy the three dates they had shared after that. But after one fatal date when there had been a mix-up in the arrangements and he had arrived half an hour early and had had to be entertained by the twins, he hadn't asked her out again.

'He's engaged now,' Annabel told her. 'I thought at one time he seemed pretty keen on you . . .'

'Obviously you were wrong.'

'You're a fool, Beatrice. You're never going to get married until you get rid of that selfish family of yours.'

Stifling her resentment, and telling herself that Annabel couldn't help her lack of tact, Beatrice responded reasonably, 'I'm quite happy as I am. I'm not looking for a husband.'

'Nonsense! You were made for marriage,' Annabel told her, 'but you need someone who'll appreciate you—spoil you—and protect you from the rest of the Bellaire clan.'

Beatrice was glad that the meal was over. There were occasions when Annabel's outspokenness could be something of a trial.

As they said their goodbyes, it struck her that, lately, she was more on edge, less resilient to life's small pinpricks. And she suspected she knew exactly where to lay the blame for that. It was Elliott who was causing her to feel as though she had one skin too few, whose constant presence filled her with a nervous tension that was beginning to overflow into every channel of her life.

She was dreading tonight, for instance. She had absolutely nothing to wear for a smart dinner party, and that was the least of her problems.

Then why not go and buy something? a treacherous inner voice suggested. She wasn't far from Knightsbridge, and Jon had told her to take the rest of the afternoon off since, apparently, he had several matters to discuss with his agent, including his timetable for the next twelve months, and so would inevitably be tied up for the rest of the day.

Without actually making the decision to do so, she found herself walking in the direction of the Knightsbridge shops, starting to window-gaze every so often. The prices stunned her and she had to blink once or twice to make sure she wasn't seeing things, but in Harvey Nichols, whose ambiance she liked because nothing was ever hurried or crowded, she found a suit that she fell in love with straight away, and which she probably would never have dared to try on if the assistant hadn't persuaded her to.

In fine wool gabardine, it had a straight, very dark navy skirt and an acid yellow jacket that picked out the red highlights in her hair and was cut in such a fashion that it enhanced her narrow waist and fitted snugly over the curve of her hips.

The jacket was collarless with a deep V-neck that the assistant assured her was perfectly respectable when worn without a blouse, especially for evening engagements. It wasn't even too expensive, so she couldn't reject it on those grounds, Beatrice admitted dolefully as she changed back into her comfortable Jaeger pleated skirt and jumper.

In Harvey Nichols she didn't look out of place in such an outfit, even though it was three years old. In fact many of the other female customers were dressed in very similar clothes, even if the majority of them were a good twenty years her senior.

'We have a very attractive selection of costume jewellery and pretty tights on the ground floor,' the assistant suggested when the suit was paid for and parcelled, and somehow, even though she had not had any such intentions originally, Beatrice found herself buying not only tights and a Chanel-style rope of pearls to fill the neckline of her suit, but also a pair of soft kid pumps in the same dark navy as her suit.

With both her energy and her bank account seriously depleted, she headed for home, surprised to discover that she had barely left herself enough time to get ready, and additionally that not once during her shopping spree had she given the slightest thought to the needs of the other members of her family. In the past such shopping expeditions as she had been able to make on her own behalf had been hurried, tense affairs, when she had ended up buying the first thing that came to hand so that she could rush home and make sure that nothing catastrophic had happened in her absence.

A rather cool silence greeted her when she walked into the kitchen. The expense of a taxi had seemed justified in view of the time, and she was still recovering from the shock of how much it had cost as she opened the kitchen door.

'I thought you had the afternoon off,' commented Ben rather truculently as she walked in.

'Yes, I did, but I had lunch with Annabel and then I decided to do some shopping. Why? Is something wrong?' Beatrice asked worriedly, the possible dire consequences of her self-indulgent afternoon suddenly catching up with her.

'No, nothing at all,' Henrietta told her calmly. 'It's just himself here, getting into a fine state because he can't find his dress-shirt.' She made it sound as though Benedict was about three years old and sulking over the absence of some highly prized and emotionally necessary garment.

'It's in the bottom drawer of your cupboard,' Beatrice told him. 'Don't you remember, you told me to put it there after the last time you wore it so that you'd remember where it was.'

It was obvious that Benedict was not appeased, and she felt her spirits begin to drop. She had feared all along that the dinner party would be likely to be a fraught occasion, and now she was being proved right.

Elliott was meeting them at the restaurant—a necessary precaution to ensure that nothing went wrong, he had claimed when Beatrice had accused him of cowardice.

Despite the fact that they would be eating later, William had insisted on having a full tea. Beatrice sat down and had a cup of coffee with him while the others went upstairs to get ready.

'Elliott's up to something,' he pronounced, thoroughly startling her. She put her coffee cup down, hoping that William hadn't seen her sudden tremor of shock.

'What . . . what do you mean?' she asked.

'It's obvious. Why else would he be taking us all out to dinner?'

'It's his birthday,' Beatrice protested, suddenly feeling extremely guilty as she remembered that she hadn't bought him a present.

'No, it's not,' William returned calmly. 'His birthday's in November—he's a Scorpio.' He gave her a sidelong look, and added thoughtfully, 'You're Taurus, aren't you? That means that the two of you are sexually compatible. We're doing astrology as part of our General Studies course,' he added kindly. 'It's supposed to give us a broader view of life, that kind of thing.'

'I . . . I think you must have made a mistake,' Beatrice said weakly.

'Not me. It's nothing to do with me. It's all written in the stars.'

'I mean about Elliott's birthday,' she told him, annoyed. 'It can't be in November.'

'Well, it is. But don't worry, I shan't give him away.' He picked up another scone, split it open and buttered it lavishly. 'Do you know, Henry is almost as good a cook as you, Bea...'

'Henry!' Beatrice closed her eyes in supplication. 'Don't let her hear you calling her that,' she warned him.

As she went upstairs to get changed she wondered if William was right. He normally was, which meant that Elliott had invented his birthday as an excuse to put into action his plan for detaching Lucilla from her producer.

As she remembered the fuss she always made of each and every member of her family's birthdays, including Lucilla—cake, cards, special party meals, presents, all the family commanded to be present— even enduring charades afterwards—Beatrice felt a wave of sadness, not untinged with guilt, wash over her. How could it have happened that no one apart from William knew that it wasn't really Elliott's birthday?

As she got to the top of the stairs, Mirry emerged from her bedroom and nearly cannoned into her.

'Help, I need a pair of black tights! Have you got any?'

She had, a replacement pair for the ones Mirry had given her, but by the time she had found and handed them over, there was even less time left to get ready, and worse, she could hear William protesting that his dinner-suit jacket was too tight.

At last they were all ready and assembled downstairs. Looking at her family as she hurried to join them, Beatrice stifled a faint stab of envy. They were each in their different ways so startlingly physically attractive—she felt like a small brown wren let loose in a cage of brightly plumaged parakeets.

'Come on, otherwise we're going to be late!'

Somehow they all managed to cram into two cars, Lucilla sulking because the skirts of her silk chiffon dress were being crushed. She glanced sneeringly at Beatrice's outfit as she got into the car, but, on her other side, Mirry tugged on her arm and whispered,

'I like it. It makes you look stunningly curvy and sexy!'

Which was more alarming than reassuring, Beatrice decided as she digested her youngest sister's remark.

They arrived at the restaurant on time. Elliott came out to greet them, and managed under the guise of ushering them all inside to murmur to Beatrice, 'It's OK. They're both here, but I want to make sure that Lucilla doesn't catch sight of them until we're all sitting down.'

They had been given a table in the centre of the small restaurant, and to judge from the expression on the face of the beaming proprietor Elliott was a favoured and welcome guest.

A little to her surprise Beatrice found that she was seated on Elliott's right, and across the width of the large round table she saw that Benedict was frowning darkly as he perceived these arrangements.

As though he read the uncertainty of her own personal thoughts, Elliott bent his head and murmured against her ear, 'Benedict is going to make a spectacular Othello one of these days.'

At last they were all seated. Menus were handed round and after a great deal of deliberation orders given.

Beatrice wasn't the only one who had neglected to bring Elliott a gift, she realised, and she frowned a little, realising on a swift pang of sadness how carelessly selfish her family could be. Was that her fault? But before she could dwell too much on her thoughts their first course was arriving.

While she realised that the food was delicious, she was too tense to enjoy it. So far, Elliott's bulk had shielded from Lucilla the sight of the couple sitting in the far corner, and she shuddered inwardly, imagining Lucilla's reaction once that shield was removed.

Elliott waited until they were half-way through their main course before making his move.

The clatter of a dropped fork on the marble floor drew Lucilla's attention, and as he bent to retrieve the object before any of the hovering waiters could do so, she had a clear view of the occupants of that secluded corner table, their attention also drawn by the intrusive noise.

Beatrice's tender heart ached for her half-sister as she saw her face change and the realisation of what she was witnessing dawn there.

Lucilla's full red lips compressed, her dark blue Bellaire eyes shooting dangerous temper sparks.

For one blissfully relieved moment Beatrice thought that that was all that was going to happen, and then abruptly Lucilla stood up and before anyone could stop her she walked over to the other couple and to Beatrice's consternation picked up the plate of food that her lover was eating and dropped its contents into his lap.

Her fury hadn't abated in the slightest when she came back. Pushing Beatrice aside she said bitterly to Elliott, 'I suppose you arranged all this, didn't you? Well I hope you're satisfied.'

'If you'd listened to reason in the first place, none of this would be necessary—but then of course you're a Bellaire,' he added with fine irony, 'and no Bellaire worthy of the name ever listens to anyone else.'

To her shock, Beatrice heard William chortle appreciatively.

'William!' she began reproachfully, but her youngest brother cut her off, saying good-humouredly, 'He's right, Bea, and you know it. Lord, but did you *see* his face?'

'He was going to give me a part in his new series!' Lucilla burst out furiously.

Elliott only looked amused, his voice faintly scathing as he drawled, 'Come on, Lu, no histrionics, please...and wouldn't it have been rather an extortionate price to pay?'

Lucilla stiffened. 'What do you mean? If you're talking about the fact that we're lovers ...'

'Oh, hardly,' drawled Elliott. He glanced mean-ingfully at the other table. 'I was referring to your inheritance, Lucilla, not your body. As the old say-ing goes, pretty women come a dime a dozen, but money—well, that's something else, and he does have very expensive tastes!'

Beatrice was making the extraordinary discovery that Lucilla did not always look beautiful. When she was angry her eyes became unpleasantly small, and her face was burning with hot colour that clashed relentlessly with her scarlet dress.

'That and the cost in terms of your pride,' Elliott added gently.

At her side Beatrice heard William give a sound-less whistle of appreciation and murmur, 'Game, set and match to Elliott. That was really neat!'

Over in the corner waiters fussed and the hum of conversation momentarily silenced by Lucilla's re-taliatory action now rose again.

Out of the corner of her eye Beatrice saw the producer and his lover get up and leave, but Lucilla was too busy arguing hotly with Elliott to notice.

Much to her surprise, Beatrice discovered that they weren't asked to leave themselves. The pro-prietor of the restaurant was Italian, Elliott ex-plained drily to her, observing her covert and anxious looks in the direction of the door into the kitchens, and therefore used to such emotional dis-plays.

Benedict, who had become very thoughtful and withdrawn after Lucilla's outburst against Elliott, now suggested that they should order a bottle of champagne to celebrate Lucilla's return to sanity, and it took quite some time to subdue the resultant outbreak of hostilities.

Benedict and Lucilla were surprisingly alike in temperament, Beatrice observed, surprised that she had never noticed before how similar Lucilla's acid remarks often were to Benedict's more skilled but just as cruel barbs. It was a disquieting discovery and one that made her look rather thoughtfully at her eldest brother.

Benedict was the image of their father, and it struck her for the first time that because of that she had perhaps invested him with virtues that he did not possess. Their father, while feckless, had always been an open-hearted, generous man. Benedict . . . Benedict had a darker side to his nature, she recognised now, a driven obsessiveness about certain things that he shared with Lucilla.

They had reached the coffee stage before Lucilla grew tired of venting her wrath on Elliott. She was quiet for several minutes and then turned to Beatrice and said acidly,

'I suppose you're the one who's responsible for this. I suppose you went crawling to Elliott to tell him how much you disapproved of Don . . .

'Poor Elliott,' she went on maliciously, glancing at her half-brother. 'Was it very difficult holding her at bay? Inexperienced virgins of a certain age can be such an embarrassment, can't they, darling? Honestly, I sometimes wonder what on earth Bea's going to drag home next, she's so obviously man-hungry. You won't get what you want from Elliott, darling,' she told Beatrice with a venomous purr. 'He's very choosy about the quality of the ladies he takes to bed. And the embargoes he sees fit to place on the rest of us don't, it seems, apply to himself. What happened to Sally Frenchman, Elliott? She was positively all over you the last time I saw her. Did her husband finally object?'

Nothing would be achieved by giving in to her desire to just get up and simply run, Beatrice told herself, gritting her teeth together resolutely, but it was hard to convince herself that Lucilla was simply acting out of chagrin and pain, and that her barbs really had nothing personal in them, save for an instinctive reflex to hurt someone more vulnerable than she was herself, but none of that helped her to deal with the growing sensation of nausea clawing at her stomach, and when Lucilla added savagely, 'Look, Bea's even bought a new outfit for you, Elliott. Where on earth did you buy it, Bea?' she purred to Beatrice. "It looks positively vile! You know your figure is far too top-heavy for you to draw attention to it like that, and besides, Elliott is a legs man, aren't you, darling?'

It was awful...unendurable...horrible...and the more so because Lucilla's taunts held just enough hint of the truth for her to feel appallingly conscious of what a complete fool she was making of herself. She *had* bought the outfit for tonight, and at the back of her mind *had* been the thought that Elliott would see her in it and perhaps...perhaps what? Indulge her in a repeat performance of those moments in his car when his mouth had... She gagged on the sickness rising inside her, but knew that she couldn't give in to it. To do so would be to reinforce the truth underlying

Lucilla's bitchy remarks, and so she had to sit there and smile calmly, and pretend she thought Lucilla's comments sprang from nothing more than her own hurt pride.

In the end, surprisingly, it was Elliott himself who stopped it, his voice cool, but holding a steely underlying thread of savagery that made Beatrice's face burn as it told her how little he relished being connected with her, even in so remote a context.

'Pull yourself together, Lucilla,' he ordered his half-sister. 'Or isn't making a fool of yourself once tonight enough? And while you're at it you can apologise to Beatrice.'

'What for?' Lucilla demanded sulkily, at least acceding to his first demand. 'Telling the truth?'

'You wouldn't know the truth if it got up and bit you,' Elliott told her sardonically.

Her nausea was starting to retreat, Beatrice discovered thankfully. For the first time since Lucilla had started on her outburst, she felt strong enough to remove her gaze from the point where she had fixed it on the restaurant wall and look at something human.

Mirry was the first one to catch her eye, and she gave her a sympathetic grimace that bolstered her overstrung nerves.

Somehow Beatrice was aware that both Benedict and Elliott were looking at her, but she couldn't bring herself to glance in either direction.

Elliott was speaking again, his voice dry and very controlled as he said suavely, 'Oh, and by the way, Lucilla, for your information, two points. The first is that Sally Frenchman is simply the wife of a friend, nothing more, and if I find you spreading gossip about her, I promise you I'll make sure you regret it.'

'And the second?' Lucilla demanded angrily, holding her head at a challenging angle as Elliot paused.

'And the second,' he told her, catching Beatrice's unwary eyes, and giving her an extremely quizzical and amused look, 'is that you're quite wrong about my sexual preferences—legwise, that is.'

Before signalling to the fascinated audience of hovering waiters, he glanced thoughtfully and extremely deliberately at the décolleté neckline of Beatrice's suit jacket, and there, in front of them all, he allowed his interested glance to make a leisurely and thorough inspection of her feminine curves, before adding softly, 'Quite definitely wrong.'

Beatrice couldn't bear to look at anyone. Inside she felt as though she was being torn apart by pain and humiliation. How *could* Elliott have done that to her? What on earth had he hoped to achieve? From someone else, such behaviour would have been gallant, but Elliott knew her and her family too well to suppose they would ever be deceived by such a display.

All of them right down to William knew of their mutual antagonism, and all that Elliott's behaviour now would have done would have been to raise unwanted speculation concerning her own feelings towards him. Beatrice knew that as well as she knew her own name, and she was bitterly convinced that

Elliott knew it as well. Given that, his actions were those of an extremely cruel and vindictive man—and yet, for all the antipathy that existed between them, she had always considered that Elliott thought of himself as above such petty behaviour as afflicted the rest of the human race.

Somehow she managed to endure the last half-hour of the dinner party, but at last she was free to get up and go.

Just as she was about to join Mirry and Benedict by the door, Elliott caught hold of her arm and, in full view of the whole family, said caressingly, looking at her but speaking to them, 'I'll bring Beatrice home.'

She ought to have refused to go with him, but he had caught her off guard and, other than wrenching her arm out of his grip, there was no way she could get away from his side.

The Bellaire clan had caused enough emotional fireworks for one night, she decided tiredly, and besides, what did it really matter who drove her home? The damage had already been done. Tonight Lucilla had held up to her own inspection and that of her family a cruel mirror image, and one that would haunt her for a long time to come. She still flinched when recalling Lucilla's gibe about her virginity. She could have pointed out that at the time when other girls her age were experimenting with sex, she had been bringing up a family, but in her own heart she knew that that defence was weak, and that somewhere deep inside her she still clung to the foolish feminine myth of the dashing prince who would come to claim her and awaken her with the magic of his kiss.

Childish daydreams that ought to have been discarded years ago, she derided herself, as the others left and Elliott paid the bill.

She was stiff with resentment and misery when they got outside, and Elliott's calm, 'Don't let Lucilla get to you. She's hurt and like any wounded creature her pain makes her want to lash out, preferably in the direction of someone weaker and more vulnerable than she is herself,' didn't help. Only by taking a deep breath and holding it in her lungs was she able to keep her voice even.

'Yes, I am able to work that out for myself, Elliott.'

'Mm... Well, if it's not Lucilla, who's made you so tense and on edge? It must be me.'

'How observant of you!' Now her voice did tremble, her attempt at sounding sarcastic woefully ineffective.

'My car's over this way.' Elliott took hold of her arm, guiding her down a narrow alley to a small side street.

Although she was aching to ask him just exactly what he had been trying to do by implying that he found her...her body...sexually desirable, Beatrice doubted that she had the self-control to do so. One betraying memory of how it had felt to be touched and caressed by him would be enough to tear apart any fiction of cool uninterest she might try to weave, and her voice would be the first thing to betray her—she knew it.

She steeled herself against flinching as Elliott handed her into his car. It was folly to have given in so easily. She ought to have insisted on going home with the others... Round and round her thoughts swarmed like tired moths beating their wings against a hot flame.

She tensed as Elliott got into the car and started the engine. Immediately her senses were swamped by the proximity and the maleness of him. She could smell his soap, see the muscles tensing in his thigh as he changed gear. Even without looking at him she was intimately aware of how the soft cotton of his shirt would cling to his torso, of how his hair grew thickly into the nape of his neck, of how his jaw would feel in the morning when he needed a shave.

She shivered convulsively, appalled by the direction of her wayward thoughts. Lucilla was right, she accepted with self-disgust; her awareness of Elliott was beginning to take on an almost farcical quality. She reminded herself of the classic spinster aunt of the family in hot pursuit of an unfortunate and unwilling victim.

It was an ugly picture, one which made her squeeze her eyes tightly closed on a wave of anguished remorse. She didn't really desire Elliott... she couldn't. She didn't even like him. But when she opened her eyes and looked at him, the pulse leaping hotly through her body couldn't be ignored.

'I'm sorry if you were embarrassed by what Lucilla said tonight, Bea.'

Her mouth tightened, her emotions caught half-way between pain and rage.

'What's the matter? Not sulking, are you?'

He was reducing her to the status of a spoiled child. Her fingers clenched in her lap and she felt tears sting her eyes.

'No one would have paid any attention to what Lucilla said if you hadn't...' She stopped abruptly, already aware that she had said too much, but instead of prompting her to go on Elliott said softly, '*You* did.'

Beneath the softness was a definite challenge, and her pride urged her that it was one she could not...must not ignore.

Fighting against the cramping sensation of panic seizing her insides, she began unsteadily, 'I...'

'I do know why you've been avoiding me so assiduously lately, you know, Bea, but there's really no need.'

That he dared to say that to her now, heaping further humiliation on top of what she had already endured, was too much. Did he really think she was stupid enough to believe that he was genuinely attracted to her, that he had genuinely wanted the sensation of her skin beneath his hands? She made a small, almost animal-like moan of pain under her breath and protested huskily, 'I'm not avoiding you. I...'

'Then prove it to me. Have lunch with me on Saturday.'

She couldn't hide her sudden start of shock, her eyes instinctively lifting to his face, as though somehow she would read something in his expression that would confirm that this was all some kind of crazy joke.

She realised she ought to have known better. Elliott was adept at not giving his feelings or thoughts away. He glanced briefly at her, a humorous, almost indulgent smile lifting his mouth.

'Poor Bea! You don't know what to think, do you? You've been conditioned too long and too well. Well?'

He couldn't be serious. It was a joke...a trap. Her face burned as she imagined him laughing with Lucilla over her gullibility.

'I...' Her mind scrabbled desperately for a dignified excuse. 'I...'

She heard Elliott laugh softly.

'What are you so afraid of, Bea?'

'Not you.' The hot, adolescent denial was voiced before she could check it, and as he looked away from her she thought she saw an amused and satisfied smile curve his mouth.

'Then have lunch with me,' he said softly, 'and prove it.' He gave her a sidelong look. 'Unless of course you're scared that Lucilla's right.'

She felt her colour rise along with her temper and said rashly, 'Don't be ridiculous!'

'Good, so it's agreed. On Saturday we're having lunch together. Where would you like to go?'

She felt literally tongue-tied, and knew she had been driven into a baited trap by an expert hunter. But why? She risked a glance into his face, and saw that he was still looking amused.

'I...'

'You'd prefer to leave it to me. Wise girl.'

It was a very weak protest, especially in view of the fact that she ought to have been telling him there was no way she would have lunch with him on Saturday, or any other day.

The corners of his mouth twitched, and Beatrice felt aware of heat scorching her body as he stopped the car and looked his leisurely fill of her.

She had been so infuriated, so engrossed, that she hadn't even realised they were home, and as she reached out to fumble with the door handle, he covered her hand with his own and leaned towards her. She tensed, remembering the previous occasion she had been alone in his car with him. Appallingly her body remembered it too, and beneath their covering of wool and lace she felt the unmistakable and provocative response of her breasts to his closeness.

He seemed to fill the car, snatching the air from her lungs and making it hard for her to breathe. He wasn't that close to her, but the warm musky scent of his body seemed to engulf her, affecting her in the most peculiar way.

Lucilla was right, she decided miserably; she was a frustrated spinster, an apology for a woman who went weak at the knees and melted inside just because a member of the opposite sex sat close to her. But as hard as she berated herself, her brain provided her with irreproachable examples of her imperviousness to any number of men, thus heightening her sense of danger to the point where she could hardly breathe for the dread pursuing her.

'Something wrong?'

The dulcet question, quite unmistakably edged with the same amusement that had curved his mouth earlier, set further alarm bells ringing.

For some reason Elliott was amused by her. No doubt the fact that she was inexperienced and undesirable amused him, she raged impotently. No doubt he enjoyed making fun of her . . . humiliating her . . .

'I . . . Why did you pretend it was your birthday?' she asked him, and was immediately furious with herself because that was not what she had intended to say at all.

The laughter died out of his eyes and the look he gave her was an odd one. If she hadn't known better she might almost have supposed that emotionally he was moved by the fact that she had known it wasn't his birthday.

She blinked, convinced that she was beginning to see things, and heard him say,

'I didn't realise you knew.'

For some reason it had become imperative to tell him that not only hadn't she known, but also that she hadn't cared to know.

'I didn't. William told me. He's been doing astrology at school . . . Scorpio and Taurus are compatible, he says.' She broke off her disjointed sentence, appalled by the reckless direction of her own thoughts, and then realised that Elliott was looking at her rather grimly, almost as though she had disappointed him in some way.

'Ah, I see. William . . . Now there's a Bellaire who makes one think there's still hope for the human race,' he commented obliquely, leaning so close to her that she automatically pressed herself back into the seat to preserve some space between them, and then she felt the door give and realised foolishly that he had simply been opening it for her.

'You two took your time getting back,' Benedict commented suspiciously when they walked in. 'What happened? Did you run out of petrol?'

Beatrice coloured and looked at him pleadingly, but Elliott seemed completely unmoved by his crass comment.

'I never run out of petrol, Benedict,' he responded lazily. 'It smacks too much of bad planning. The female sex, especially when it's being seduced, does not as a rule take kindly to bad planning. A fact I see you have yet to discover,' he added with a kindly avuncularity that brought a dark frown to Benedict's eyes.

Sebastian grinned appreciatively. 'He's got you outmanoeuvred there, brother dear!'

William, who had helped himself to a slice of plum cake which he was stuffing into his mouth, paused long enough to say through a mouthful of crumbs, 'Elliott could run rings round Ben any day of the week.'

Why had she never noticed before that even when Elliott wasn't smiling his eyes seemed to gleam with inner humour? Beatrice wondered as she heard him gravely thanking her youngest brother for his compliment.

All in all, she was glad that the day was nearly over; and equally glad to be able to escape from her family to the peace and solitude of her own room.

Resolutely she refused to allow herself the self-indulgence of dwelling on the events of the evening, but one thing she was determined upon. She would find out exactly why Elliott was trying to give the impression that he was interested in her as a woman. There was some purpose behind it, there had to be. She was not so foolish as to be taken in by him, and she would discover exactly what that purpose was, she told herself. In fact, that was the only reason she had agreed to have lunch with him.

Feeling much better, she dismissed her earlier feeling of vulnerability, not to say fear that she was dangerously responsive to the maleness of Elliott in a way that showed her that she was not as impervious to sexual desire and love as she had always supposed.

Love? For Elliott Chalmers? How ridiculous! And yet . . . and yet . . .

Thoroughly frightened, she stopped what she was doing. Of course she didn't love Elliott. How could she? But something deep inside her refused to be reassured.

CHAPTER SIX

ON Wednesday Beatrice was frantically busy typing out the schedules Jon had brought back with him from his agent. Several phone calls during the day meant alterations in them, and by three o'clock in the afternoon she felt exhausted.

There was an empty block of six weeks in the middle of the schedules, and when she queried this Jon explained that he was already contracted to spend that period in Italy working in Florence with a small but renowned opera company.

She had only been working for Jon for a matter of days, but already she was beginning to enjoy herself and she wondered what she would be supposed to do while he was in Italy. Although he was as vague and demanding as a small child, looking after one man as compared with looking after her entire volatile family was a sinecure. She had always loved music, but before there had never really been any time for her to develop that love. Now she found, listening to Jon playing while she worked in the adjoining study, her interest deepening and growing.

The theatre exclusively dominated the lives of her brothers and sisters. Music was part of that world, but not its centre. At school she had once been told she had a pretty voice, and now she found herself wishing it was stronger, and that she had at least one artistic gift that could match the cornucopia of talents showered down upon her family.

She was so busy at work she barely had time to notice Benedict's sulks, or Lucilla's dramatics. It was Henrietta who told her that Lucilla had announced that she was going to move out of the Wimbledon house and find her own flat, and, to her surprise, Beatrice found she really did not particularly care. In the past, whenever Lucilla had thrown that particular gauntlet at her, she had been motivated by guilt and responsibility into pleading with her to stay, her pleas all the more intense because inwardly she felt that there was nothing she would like more than for Lucilla's turbulent presence to be removed from the house. But Lucilla was in a way as much her responsibility as the others, and she had never been able to escape thinking that her father would have wanted and expected her to keep Lucilla within the shelter of the family home.

Now, when she listened to Henrietta's news, she simply nodded, and said that Lucilla was old enough to make her own decisions.

'Now that's exactly what I said,' Henrietta approved, 'and unless I miss my mark that young lady is well aware which side her bread's buttered. Take it from me, when she realises that no one's going to pay any attention to her little tantrum, she'll soon change her tune, but Master Ben would have it that you'd raise heaven and earth to get her to stay. He even seemed to think you'd blame Master Elliott for her leaving... seemed to relish the idea too, although heaven knows why.' She glanced thoughtfully at Beatrice's set face and added placidly, 'Well,

I suppose it's bound to put his nose out of joint a little bit, having Master Elliott living here, when he's been used to considering himself the head of the family.' She chuckled indulgently as though Benedict was no more than five years old, and indeed, Beatrice thought guiltily, sometimes her brother reminded her more of a sulky child than a fully grown adult.

She hadn't told anyone about her Saturday lunch date. Part of her was hoping Elliott would forget, or that by some miraculous means the rest of the family would disappear on Saturday morning, thus ensuring that no one other than herself was aware of her folly.

She hoped in vain.

Over supper Benedict barely spoke, and when she cautiously asked Sebastian afterwards if anything was wrong, he shook his head.

'No, he's just put out about you going out for lunch with Elliott on Saturday.'

'He . . . he knows about that?'

'Yes,' Sebastian told her carelessly. 'Elliott mentioned it when Ben asked him if he could borrow his car. He said he wasn't going to risk taking you out to lunch in Ben's in case it ran out of petrol.' Sebastian grinned down at her. 'I'll leave you to imagine the rest. Elliott's right, you know, you spoil us all dreadfully,' he added obliquely.

Although Benedict didn't say a word to her, Beatrice was intensely conscious of the atmosphere pervading the sitting-room when she walked in.

Benedict and Elliott were playing chess.

Benedict played it as he did everything, with verve, skill and showmanship. Elliott's moves were quieter, more studied ... and deadlier, Beatrice noticed, biting her lip anxiously as she watched Elliott take yet another of Benedict's pawns.

It struck her quite forcibly, watching them, that there was more to the game than seemed initially obvious. It was as though Benedict was deliberately challenging Elliott. But over what, and why?

She crinkled her forehead as she tried to remember if there had been any animosity between the two of them in the past. Apart from Elliott's refusal to buy Benedict an expensive car, there was nothing. No, it was only since Elliott had been living with them that this odd antagonism seemed to have sprung to life. Until recently she had thought she was the only member of the family who felt prickly and defensive in Elliott's presence. It came as rather a shock to realise that her self-assured brother was on the defensive, and she looked at Elliott with new eyes.

At that very moment he looked up himself, and the way he looked at her made her feel acutely odd. Her legs seemed to have lost all their muscle tone, her stomach felt weak and achy, and her head buzzed as though she was about to faint. She fought off the sensation, frightened by it. She seemed to be frightened all the time these days, and Elliott was at the root of that fear.

Not for the first time she wished she had never allowed herself to be so foolishly trapped into having lunch with him, but she sensed that she would not be allowed to wriggle out of it now.

Saturday arrived far too quickly. The moment she woke up, Beatrice felt burdened by an acute awareness of apprehension. A childish desire to burrow beneath her quilt and put off the evil hour by going back to sleep made her wriggle guiltily in the warmth of her bed. It was sheer luxury not to have to get up and race downstairs in order to start preparing everyone's breakfasts.

Elliott had introduced a new rule that anyone wanting an early breakfast on weekend mornings had to prepare their own, adding smoothly, before anyone could object, that Henrietta was not as young as she had been and deserved a weekend rest.

Much to Beatrice's amazement, no one had pointed out that Beatrice was there to take over from their new housekeeper. Elliott had the knack of making her family toe the line, she admitted resentfully, while inwardly acknowledging that, with Elliott as a father, her brothers, especially Benedict, would have benefited a great deal from his calm firmness.

Elliott as a father? What dangerous byways were her thoughts leading her down now?

She jumped out of bed and discovered that the sun was shining from a perfect cloudless sky. The impropriety of leaning out of her bedroom window wearing nothing other than her fine cotton nightdress was forcibly imposed on her when she happened to glance down into the garden and saw that Elliott was standing there looking up at her.

To her chagrin she blushed furiously and stepped back from the window. As she dressed, she prayed that no one else had observed or heard his soft laughter. What was he trying to do to her?

Trying to do? an inner voice demanded scornfully. He had already done it. He had made her conscious of him as a very male man in a way she had previously never believed possible. It was a line of thought she didn't want to pursue, so instead she brushed her hair vigorously and wondered rather grimly how he would like taking out a woman who looked as plain and uninteresting as she did.

She had no idea where he was taking her for lunch and certainly had no intention of asking him, but her wardrobe was woefully short of smart clothes, and she was most certainly not going to wear the yellow and navy again.

Her only other 'expensive' and suitable outfit was a dull silk dress she had bought for a friend's wedding. The dark cream fabric did absolutely nothing for her colouring, while its shapeless fit chosen to conceal her shape had the effect of making her look distinctly matronly, she decided critically.

Mirry came in while she was studying herself, and confirmed her opinion by saying, 'Where on earth did you get that? It's dreadful!'

'It's silk, and it was expensive,' protested Beatrice.

She saw that her sister was carrying a small tissue-wrapped parcel which she put down on the bed.

'Look, why don't I lend you something,' Mirry began, but Beatrice shook her head.

'We both know I'd never get into anything of yours. What's that?' she asked, looking at the small parcel.

'Oh, it's something one of the other girls made. She wanted that red dress I made—remember?—so I swapped her this for it, but it isn't really me; it's too big, so I thought I'd give it to you. What do you think?'

Miranda shook out the tissue and Beatrice stared at the wisp of peach silk she held up in her hands.

'It's a pair of camiknickers,' Mirry explained when she didn't make any comment. 'Don't you like it? I thought it was very you.'

Beatrice could see what it was, but she had been lost for words at the thought of wearing anything quite so provocative. Tiny thin straps supported the ethereal garment, satin buttons with loops marched all the way down the front; delicate butterflies appliquéd in slightly darker silk formed the cups which Beatrice felt sure would never support her too generous breasts, and when Mirry swirled it round so that she could see the back she gasped to see how low it dipped. Another silky butterfly formed all that there was of the bottom half of the back, and Beatrice blinked bemusedly as she realised how exceedingly provocative it would look when worn.

'You'll need to wear stockings with it, of course,' Mirry told her, showing her where the tiny delicate suspenders were concealed, talking as matter-of-factly as though her wearing of such a garment was an everyday event.

'Mirry, I can't wear anything like that. I'd . . . I'd look ridiculous,' she protested uncertainly, feeling as hurt as a small child.

'No, you wouldn't, you'd look . . . sexy,' Mirry told her stalwartly, adding with a quickly surprised grin, 'I bet Elliott would think so!'

To Mirry it was all a game; she didn't mean to hurt. She was so confident of her own allure that it never occurred to her that others might feel less secure. And what could she say without risking betraying herself?

'I . . .' Beatrice could see that Mirry was disappointed by her response, and realised guiltily that her sister had quite genuinely hoped to please her with her gift. 'It's . . . lovely,' she said at last, reaching out to touch the shimmering fabric.

'I knew you'd love it. That's why . . .'

Beatrice saw Mirry bite her lip, and realised that the story of the 'swap' had possibly been an invention and that Mirry had intended all along for the camiknickers to belong to her. How could she refuse them and hurt her sister's feelings?

'Look, I've even got you a pair of stockings, because I know you never wear them.' She produced them from within the folds of the tissue with a flourish. 'Real silk!'

A lump solidified in Beatrice's throat. 'I . . .' she began.

Mirry hugged her impulsively, and whispered,

'Don't let Ben get you down. He can be a menace at times... God, is that the time? I've got to run, I'm meeting Jane and Susie at eleven. Have a nice day!'

She was alone, and there was no one to see her or laugh at her as she reached out and tremulously touched the soft silk. It felt alive and warm beneath her fingertips, and she had a momentary traitorous desire to know what such a fabric would feel like against her skin.

She looked at the garment and then glanced away, as though trying to avoid temptation, and then looked back again. She would look ridiculous in it, of course, but there could be no harm in just trying it on. Mirry had meant what she said about it suiting her, and, whatever else she might not have, when it came to clothes, Mirry had a definite 'eye'.

Her bedroom had its own bathroom, and quite ridiculously she took the precaution of locking its door behind her as she went inside.

Her fingers actually trembled as she unfastened her dress, and out of habit she avoided looking at her reflection as she stripped off her clothes. All her adult life she had been conditioned to think of her body as ugly because it did not fit into the accepted Bellaire mode.

It wasn't particularly that she was fat, just that her overall shape was wrong . . . her breasts too full, her waist ludicrously narrow for such fullness, the curve of her hips too lush, too rounded. Her legs were all right, she acknowledged grudgingly, but they weren't long enough . . . even if her ankles were slimmer than Lucilla's.

That thought amazed her. When had she noticed that, despite her overall slenderness, Lucilla had rather thick ankles?

Somehow, in the midst of thinking all this, she had slipped on the peach silk. She fastened the buttons tremulously, surprised to discover that discreetly inserted beneath the butterflies was just sufficient underwiring to support the fullness of her breasts. And not just to support, she acknowledged, catching sight of herself and expelling her breath in a noisy rush as she saw how the peach silk enhanced her skin tones, and how that discreet underwiring flagrantly emphasised the full curves of her breasts in such a way that instead of seeming over-full they merely appeared to be tantalisingly rounded.

Completely bemused, she turned round and peered at her back view. A small 'oh' of shocked astonishment surprised from her mouth as she saw how provocatively the butterfly wings spanned the curve of her bottom and how indiscreetly they revealed it feminine roundness.

Scarcely knowing what she was doing, she sat down and slipped on the stockings. They were a soft natural shade that went with everything and which, after she had fastened the suspenders tucked discreetly under the edge of the camiknicker legs, exposed just the right amount of silky-skinned thigh.

Her appearance was a total revelation, and she kept on staring at herself as though she was looking at a stranger. There was no doubt in her mind that Mirry's friend had been given exact and correct measurements, because the garment fitted as though it had been made for her, right down to skimming the contours of her waist. And Mirry had been right, it did suit her. But that didn't mean that she was going to wear it, she decided firmly.

Her hand was on the top button when she heard someone banging on her bedroom door. Without thinking she unlocked and opened her bathroom door and snatched up a robe.

'Who is it?' she called.

'It's me, Elliott. You've got exactly five minutes to get downstairs; otherwise I'm coming in to get you, or had you forgotten we're having lunch together today?'

Five minutes! Beatrice stared in appalled horror at the closed but unlocked door. Five minutes . . .

'Four minutes,' Elliott intoned outside, and she knew he wasn't making idle threats. Four minutes! She started to panic. She'd never get out of this and dressed again in that time.

'Three minutes . . .'

In a fever of dread she snatched up her cream silk dress and tugged it on, her fingers fumbling with the buttons. At last it was fastened. The belt, where was the belt? She found it and heard Elliott saying outside, 'Two minutes . . .'

Her hair . . . She had to brush her hair, and where were her lipstick and her bag?

She made it with thirty seconds to spare, opening the door to find Elliott leaning on the wall outside. She blinked and stared as she saw that he was wearing jeans and a soft cotton shirt with the neck unfastened and the sleeves rolled up, but before she could speak, he said softly,

'Well done! You made it—just.' And then he was taking her arm and guiding her downstairs, even though every atom of common sense she had was shrieking at her to make some excuse and tell him she had changed her mind, that she wasn't going anywhere with him. Where on earth was he taking her, anyway, dressed like that? Another man would have seemed more approachable, more... more homely, dressed so casually, but with Elliott it only seemed to increase his air of dangerous masculinity.

Somehow she found that she was in his car and that the time for sane objections was gone. He got in beside her and started the engine, swinging the large car out into the late Saturday morning traffic with aplomb.

As she sat there at his side, Beatrice was beyond conversation... beyond anything apart from wondering bitterly how on earth she had allowed herself to be manoeuvred into such a situation.

They were well out of London before she came to sufficiently to ask where they were going.

Turning his head, Elliott smiled at her.

The effect of that totally natural and totally unexpected smile was devastating. Her heart flipped right over, her throat closing, a wave of knowledge washing over her that she knew would change her life for ever. She did love him. She blinked, but he was still there and so was the way she felt about him. Why had she never realised it before? Because she had deliberately hidden away behind her protective front of antipathy, she recognised; because she had firmly refused to allow herself to think of him as anything other than Lucilla's half-brother; because somewhere deep inside she had known all along that if she let her guard down, if she didn't protect herself... She couldn't love him; it was ridiculous. She would have realised it years ago. But the knowledge refused to go away. She did love him.

'There's something I want to show you. It will take us a while to get there, so you just sit back and relax.'

'You said you wanted to take me out to lunch.' Thank God he couldn't read her thoughts!

'That's right,' he agreed urbanely. 'Now just relax, there's a good girl.'

Beatrice had to bite down on her tongue to stop herself from saying churlishly that she wasn't a girl...and from demanding that he turn the car round and take her back to Wimbledon.

If she had fallen in love with him, why on earth couldn't she have realised it before now? Nothing would have induced her to spend time alone with him if she had known before how she felt. And now it was too late. She swallowed tensely. Whatever else happened, she must not let him see how she felt.

CHAPTER SEVEN

THEY were on the motorway, the M4, Beatrice observed. The miles sped by in a confused jumble of greenery and other cars, then Elliott took a turn-off. They were somewhere near the Cotswolds, Beatrice recognised numbly. It seemed rather a long way to come for lunch.

Elliott turned off the main road, and opened the sun roof; amazingly Beatrice could hear birdsong. They drove through several small villages. Her stomach rumbled protestingly, reminding her that she hadn't had any breakfast. She felt very on edge.

'Nearly there.'

She refused to look at Elliott; she dared not look at him, she admitted, knowing that the quivers in her lower body had nothing to do with any hunger for food.

They drove through yet another picturesque village, ducks swimming placidly on the river that ran alongside the road, and then Elliott turned abruptly into what was little more than a narrow lane, banked by high hedges. The lane ended abruptly in front of a pair of closed wrought-iron gates attached to brick pillars, and Beatrice winced at the thought of Elliott having to reverse all the way back. There was certainly no room to turn round anywhere, but, to her surprise, he stopped the car and got out.

As she watched he strode over to the gates and unlocked them, tucking the key back in his pocket after he had pushed them open.

'Elliott . . .' she began.

'It's all right, we're almost there.'

He seemed to be too busy concentrating on man-oeuvring the car through the gates and down the narrow drive to pay any attention to the rising note of concern in her voice, and Beatrice sighed in frustration, forced to sit and wonder where on earth he was taking her.

The drive curved sharply, and she caught her breath on a soft sound of delight as she saw the house in front of them. It lay against the backdrop of rolling fields, basking in the sun. It looked late Tudor, she decided, glancing enviously at the mullioned windows set into their stone surrounds.

It was the sort of house one expected to see full of children and dogs, a family home much loved and lived in, but as they drove up it was oddly quiet.

Beatrice turned in her seat questioningly, wondering why on earth Elliott had brought her here. There were no signs anywhere to say that it was a hotel or restaurant. No other cars . . . no other human beings . . . nothing but birdsong in the distance, and the soft sigh of the summer breeze in the ivy that clung to the walls.

'Elliott,' she began questioningly.

'Come on, out you get. All will be revealed in time. What do you want to do first?' he asked lazily, stretching as he opened her door for her. He was like a big jungle cat, she thought dizzily, watching him turn his face up to the sun, visualising the sleek ripple of muscle beneath the smoothness of his skin. 'Eat or explore?'

'Elliott, what is this place?' she demanded shakily. 'What are we doing here?' A horrid thought struck her. 'We're . . . we're not trespassing, are we? Who does this place belong to?'

He looked at her and smiled.

'Me, Beatrice. It belongs to me.'

Elliott owned this house! It gave her a jolt to realise there was so much about his life she did not know. This wasn't a bachelor's house; it was a family home. Elliott lived and worked in London. What could he possibly want with a house like this?

'You mean as . . . as an investment?' she questioned cautiously.

He shook his head.

'No, as a home. I've had enough of living in London. Oh, I shall keep the apartment—it has its uses—but I've decided it's time I started thinking about the future . . . about a family.'

She had the feeling that he was laughing at her, and she swallowed hard, suddenly tormented by a mental picture of him surrounded by dark-haired, grey-eyed children . . .

'I . . . I didn't know,' she said weakly. 'I . . . You said you were taking me out for lunch.' Her bewilderment showed in her voice, and he laughed.

'What's the matter? Frightened that I might forget to feed you? It's all taken care of. There's a picnic hamper in the boot—Henrietta packed it for me. Come and have a look inside.'

Why was he showing this house to her? Thoroughly confused . . . too confused to argue or object . . . Beatrice followed him, waiting as he unlocked the door and then ushered her inside.

The touch of his fingers on her arm made her quiver, or was it the coolness of the hallway after the heat of the sun?

The house was still furnished; it smelled of wax and pot-pourri, and she felt as though she ought to tiptoe around in case she disturbed someone. It had that air about it of being lived in which instantly appealed to her.

'The man who inherited it lives and works abroad. He didn't want to be bothered getting rid of all the furniture, so I bought the house as it stood. It belonged to his grandparents.'

He pushed open a door, and Beatrice stared into a prettily furnished drawing-room. There were three other rooms downstairs, including a small library which Elliott told her he intended to use as his study.

'I can work from here just as well as I can from London, and besides, it will give me plenty of time to spend with the children.'

Beatrice swallowed, and said faintly,

'Er, you intend to have a family, then?'

Again, he seemed to be laughing at her, and she wondered if he had guessed how unutterably miserable the thought of him married with a family had suddenly made her feel.

'Oh, I think so, don't you?' His hand on her arm guided her up the worn stairs. 'And it's close enough to Stratford for your family to come and visit us, as they will undoubtedly wish to do, if only to assure themselves that I'm not ill-treating you.'

Her head spun and she grabbed hold of the closest support, which just happened to be Elliott's
arm. They were at the top of the stairs now, on a
pleasantly square landing with several doors leading off it.

'You look faint. I think you'd better come and sit
down,' Elliott said solicitously, leading her into one
of the bedrooms.

It had a four-poster bed with pretty floral hang-
ings. A young girl's room, Beatrice decided wildly,
glancing at the matching wallpaper and the pastel
carpet.

'Elliott,' she said faintly, letting him push her
gently down on to the bed. 'What...' She swallowed painfully. 'What are you talking about?'

'I'm talking about you and me, Bella Beatrice,
and the life I hope we are going to live together.'

Her head whirled, and she wondered for a moment if she was hearing things. She looked at him
with a puzzled, bewildered little-girl look, and heard
him laugh softly.

A pain that threatened to be worse than any pain
she had endured before gathered round her heart.
How *could* he tease her like this? Didn't he know?

'Elliott, why are you doing this?' she asked him
miserably.

'Doing what?'

He was sitting down next to her, and she had to
turn slightly so that she could look at him. Motes of
dust danced in the sunlight and all around them the
old house seemed to sigh and settle as though roused
from a deep sleep.

'You know what I mean.' Her voice was low and unhappy. 'Why all the flattery and pursuit? And what you said just now...it can't be because you...you find me attractive.'

There was a brief silence and she became aware that his fingers, which moments before had tightened on hers, were now caressing her wrist, measuring the frantic pulse that beat there.

'Can't it? Why not?'

'Because I'm not the sort of woman you find attractive,' she said flatly, feeling the painful beat of her heart, and realising as she said it how much that knowledge hurt.

'You mean *you* think you're not,' he corrected. 'Certainly you don't have the brilliant plumage of the other members of the Bellaire tribe,' he agreed sardonically, 'but you're very far from being the Plain Jane you seem to consider yourself. I think that's one of the things about you that irritates me the most, Beatrice. That and the way that you let the rest of the family walk all over you. What is it, I wonder, that makes you so determined to show the world the worst side of yourself? A kind of stubborn inverted pride, I suppose. God knows where you inherited that little lot from. The rest of your family aren't exactly inclined to hide their lights under a bushel, are they?'

To her astonishment he suddenly cupped her face in his hands and leaned so close to her that she could see the dark smoky irises round his eyes.

'You have the most marvellous bone structure, a clear fine skin, and the most staggeringly feminine shape.'

She knew she was flushing hotly, and there was nothing she could do about it. She felt as though she had strayed into a strange make-believe world where nothing had any reality.

'Don't you *know* what a challenge you are to a man,' Elliott groaned softly, 'with that intriguing mixture of Earth Mother and innocent?'

'Stop it!' Beatrice jerked from him, unbearably hurt that he could mock her like this. 'I'm not a complete fool, Elliott,' she told him shakily. 'I know that men . . . at least men like you . . . don't find me attractive. I don't know why . . .'

'Do you want a man like me to find you attractive?' he interrupted in a dangerous, silky voice, that sent tremors of delicious fear shivering all through her body. 'Is it so very hard to believe that I want you . . . that I love you?' his voice whispered against her senses with hypnotic intensity. She shivered against his hands as they touched her face.

'How can you?' Her throat felt sore and rough. 'How *can* you love me? You've always seemed to dislike me . . . to be angry with me.'

'And so I was,' Elliott agreed mockingly, 'for giving your time and attention to your selfish, helpless family, when I was so obviously a far more worthy candidate for it.' He groaned suddenly, pulling her into his arms. 'God knows I'm probably just as selfish as they are, but at least I'll give you something in return.'

'Like what?' She was too bemused to take in what he was saying properly.

'Like this.' The words whispered over her skin, her insides melting on a wave of panic and delight as his mouth touched hers.

'Elliott!' She opened it to protest, but the sound was smothered beneath the fierce, dominating heat of his kiss. It was like drowning . . . like being swept into a dangerous undertow impossible to fight, and she didn't even try. She simply gave herself up to the sheer magic of it, letting him do with her what he wished.

She felt the softness of the mattress beneath her back and realised that she was lying down, with the weight of Elliott's body pressing her further into the bed.

She thought vaguely about objecting and then realised that since he could hardly really be holding her like this, kissing her like this, she must obviously be dreaming, and, since she was, there was scarcely any point in bothering to fight. Soon she would wake up, and she might as well enjoy herself until she did.

As soon as the traitorous word slid into her mind she tried to reject it. How could she enjoy herself in Elliott's embrace? How could she not? a strange, wickedly sensual side of her nature, which she had never previously known existed, demanded wantonly.

'I don't believe any of this is happening.'

She hadn't realised she had actually spoken out loud until she heard Elliott chuckle against her ear.

'Oh, it's happening all right, my love!'

'I'm not your anything,' she told him crossly in a breathless little voice she barely recognised as her own.

Her body had surrendered itself to him so quickly and so totally that her mind was still struggling with the shock of it. All these years and she had never known how she really felt about him. All those years during which her body had kept its secret so well that she had never even guessed.

'Not yet,' Elliott agreed softly, 'but you will be.'

He couldn't mean it. He was just playing with her...tormenting her. And yet under the heel of her palm his heart thudded jerkily, and his eyes, when she could bring herself to look into them, blazed nearly black with an excitement totally at odds with the lazy amusement in his voice. He looked, she recognised in bemused wonder, like a man holding himself under such a tight control that the strain of it showed in the lines of tension fanning out from his eyes and mouth.

'How can you have not known how I feel about you?'

'How could I have known?' Beatrice protested in a daze. 'You never...'

'I never what? Touched you? Kissed you?' He groaned again. 'I couldn't, not without betraying myself completely. You've gone around for so long so totally wrapped up in your damned family, that I hardly dared believe it when you finally looked at me and saw me—not as an extension of that family, but as a man.'

'When...when did I do that?' She blurted out the question, feeling her skin burn, wondering how much more she had betrayed to him. She still couldn't believe that he wasn't playing a game with her, that he wasn't going to turn round and tell her it was all a cruel joke.

'The night of Lucilla's dinner party.' His teeth nipped at her ear, his words almost drowned out in the moist sigh of his breath.

'You made me angry.'

She felt the rumble of laughter begin somewhere deep in his chest.

'I've been trying to get some sort of reaction out of you for years, but you've never even batted an eyelid, until that night.'

She swallowed, half of her aching to give in to it, and to believe implicitly in what he was saying, the other half wary, tensed to protect her against the pain of discovering it was all a lie.

'When your parents died I thought you might turn to me, but no, quite the opposite. You shut me out. But at least I had Lucilla as an excuse for seeing you.'

Closing her eyes, Beatrice remembered how often he had appeared in those agonising early weeks after her parents' death. She had assumed he was checking up on her suitability to act as Lucilla's surrogate mother. She tried to remember if there had ever been anything in his behaviour to suggest how he felt about her.

'You never showed how you felt about me,' she protested.

'And receive the same short shrift as Benedict and Co gave the rest of your suitors? I've got more sense than that, Bella Bea.'

She opened her mouth to deny his comment, and then closed it again, remembering uncertainly how those men she had brought home had drifted away. At the time she had blamed her own lack of appeal. Now... She swallowed again and looked bravely into the dark grey eyes only inches away from her.

'You're not doing this because you feel sorry for me, are you? Because of what Lucilla said the other night about...' she could feel the heat creeping over her skin... 'about my being a... a frustrated spinster?'

To her astonishment Elliott laughed.

'If I feel sorry for anyone it's myself, and as for the rest...A spinster at twenty-seven? Oh no, you're not that. I've told you before, Lucilla is jealous of you. And when it comes to being frustrated...' He paused suddenly, a peculiar gleam making his eyes glitter brilliantly as he looked at her in a way that sent quivers of sensation exploding out from the centre of her body right into her fingers and toes.

'You know I'm going to make love to you, don't you?'

Did she? Her body was reacting in a wildly abandoned way to what he was saying, but she managed to make a gurgled protest about wanting their lunch, at which Elliott laughed again, and murmured,

'In fact, I don't know how I've managed to keep my hands off you for this long! However, if you're hungry...'

Extremely ungallantly, he lifted his weight away from her and stood up, but when she made to follow, he pushed her back gently and said, 'Oh no, you stay right there. I won't be a moment.'

She knew she ought to move. It was crazy to simply languish there waiting...waiting to be made love to like an obedient puppet. She shivered and sat up, touching her forehead as though expecting to find signs of an incipient fever. What on earth was happening to her? Her whole world seemed to have turned topsy-turvy. Elliott couldn't love her, could he? She tried to think of some valid reason why he might go to such elaborate lengths to make a fool of her, but her brain refused to co-operate and she could not come up with a single one. Instead, it seemed to prefer to linger self-indulgently on what he had said, and the way he had looked at her, and she was still deep in this pleasant daydream when he came back, carrying a large picnic basket.

Her eyes widened as he kicked the door closed behind him and put the basket on the bed.

'We can't eat in here,' she protested.

'Why not?'

Beatrice opened her mouth and stared at him, unable to come up with a single reasonable objection.

'When I was little I used to pretend that my bed was a ship sailing on highly dangerous seas.'

He was opening the basket and poking about inside it with his back to her. She really ought to insist that they went downstairs. It was crazy staying up here with him. Downstairs they could talk sanely and...

'Elliott?' she began.

'Mm...chicken or salmon? Henry has packed both.'

'I...'

'Here, try the salmon, it looks delicious. Open your mouth.'

She had always been obedient as a child, and it was a habit that had stuck. He was right, the salmon was delicious, and so was its tangy sauce.

'Hold still. You've got sauce all round your mouth.'

It was an exaggeration, but as she leaned forward and his tongue stroked softly over her lips, Beatrice really didn't care. She didn't want food, she realised dizzily, she wanted him.

She'd screwed her eyes tightly closed the moment he touched her, and now she opened them, staring at him in stunned amazement.

'Chicken?' he invited softly, and all she could do was shake her head and flush softly as she saw desire leap hotly in his eyes to meet the laughter already there.

'If you get really hungry you can always nibble on me,' Elliott teased as he removed the picnic basket from the bed, but there was no amusement in his eyes as he turned back to gather her into his arms, only a hot, open need that made her stomach muscles tense in instinctive protest.

'It's all right, there's nothing to be frightened of. I'm the one who should be scared,' he murmured as he smoothed her hair back off her face and stroked his fingers against her scalp, easing the tension building up in her nerve endings. 'If I go wrong now I could lose you for ever. You've no idea how much that knowledge has tormented me down the years, how often I've ached to take hold of you and make you see me as a man.'

He was already undressing her, his fingers deft on the buttons of her dress, and then abruptly she remembered what she was wearing underneath and she grabbed the front of her dress protectively, holding it against her.

'Beatrice?' He leaned forward, stroking her mouth with the tip of his tongue until she forgot why she was hanging on to her dress and wanted only to slide her hands into his hair and hold his mouth against her own.

She made a soft sound of feminine satisfaction deep in her throat as she achieved this ambition. Part of her mind registered the fact that Elliott was sliding her dress off her shoulders, but she was too busy enjoying the delicious sensation of his mouth moving against her own to pay much attention, and Elliott was the one who tensed as he eased her dress away from her body and saw what she was wearing underneath.

Because she was watching him, she was able to see his eyes darken and shimmer with a need that made her feel almost light-headed.

It couldn't be real; this *couldn't* be Elliott looking at her like a man who had ached and hungered for the sight and feel of her so much that his need had caused him acute physical pain.

His fingers trembled as they touched the first of the tiny satin-covered buttons.

'Mirry gave it to me.'

For once he seemed to have lost that acute perception that always alarmed her. He looked at her with hot, passion-blinded eyes.

'You wore *this* for me?'

He sounded so...so humbled that she had to blink back quick tears of pain and pride. She wanted to reach out and restore to him the arrogance that was so familiar to her, and in that instant she knew how deeply she loved him.

Too deeply, an inner voice warned her, but she didn't want to listen to it. She wanted to hold to her for ever that moment when Elliott had looked at her and she had read in his eyes that he wanted her.

She tried to tell him that her choice of underwear had been dictated by circumstance rather than by choice, but his hands were moving slowly over her satin-clad breasts, causing tremors of sensation to ripple through her.

'Touch me, Beatrice.'

She wanted to resist, to tell him that she wasn't ready, but she was overwhelmed by the sudden rush of emotion sweeping over her as his hands swept back up over her body to ease down the fabric covering her breasts.

'You can't know how much I've ached to do this,' he told her softly, 'and this.'

He bent his head and she felt his lips gently caressing her breasts.

As she looked down at his dark head as it lay against her breasts she was swept by a wave of emotion so intense that it left her hot and shaking. She ached for him in every pore of her body; wanted him with a need that left no room for pride or doubt.

As he kissed his way slowly back up to her mouth she wrapped her arms round him, arching her back instinctively so that her breasts were pressed against his chest. He made a sound deep in his throat and moved his body deliberately against her, until the delicate friction made her cry out beneath his mouth and arch feverishly against him, wanting him with such an intensity that it left no room for anything else.

His mouth left hers and she knew he was looking down into her unguarded face as he deliberately aroused her. Unwillingly she opened her eyes.

'This is how I've dreamed of seeing you for years...aroused...wanting me the way I want you. And you *do* want me, don't you, Bella Bea?'

The immediate leap of her pulses, the need that burned inside her, were shocking discoveries for a woman who had always thought of herself as cool and controlled.

There was nothing controlled about her now, she admitted shakily, feeling the fine tremors building up inside her, knowing that Elliott only had to look at her to make her burn up inside.

His thumb pressed softly against her bottom lip, teasing her, and she bit at it, quivering impatiently, caught up in a tension she didn't fully understand. She caught a stifled moan and thought she had hurt him as she looked into his tortured face. She must have made some sound in response, because Elliott shook his head and said huskily, 'Shush, it's all right. I thought I could do this slowly and carefully, but it isn't going to work.' His voice was suddenly raw with a need that both excited and alarmed her. 'You're making it impossible for me to hold on to any self-control. Twenty-seven years old and with about as much experience as a seventeen-year-old, and you're driving me out of my mind!'

He moved, tugging open the rest of the satin-covered buttons almost clumsily before smoothing the fabric away from her body with hands that actually seemed to tremble... Or was she the one who trembled? she wondered achingly as she felt her body's response to his avid visual appreciation of her.

Whenever she had imagined such a moment in her life, she had believed that her embarrassment with her own nudity would be such that there would be no room for anything else. But embarrassment was the last thing on her mind as she saw the way Elliott looked at and responded to her.

In a gesture as old as time itself her body arched and invited, her curves enticing. She closed her eyes, every nerve end quivering, instinct telling her that Elliott would not be able to resist such an invitation, her breath up in her throat as she waited for the glorious heat and weight of him to descend upon her.

But nothing happened, and she opened her eyes again, her total abandonment to her own femininity retreating before an advancing tide of insecurity.

He looked back at her, holding her eyes so that she couldn't look away.

'This is your last chance to change your mind,' he told her huskily. 'If I touch you now, I'm not going to be able to stop until I've made love to you, and I warn you, Bea, that my hunger for you is going to take one hell of a lot of appeasing.'

She shivered, but it wasn't with fear, and when she held her arms to him, the look that darkened his eyes made her singingly aware of all her power as a woman.

He took her in his arms and kissed her, his mouth caressing hers with a hungry pressure that made her moan softly and ache for more. She was having difficulty dragging enough air into her lungs. She both wanted to urge him to make love to her completely, and to wait, both longing for the act of completion and nervous of it. If he could make her feel like this simply by touching her... She shuddered. Sensation after sensation ran through her body, making her ache for more than the arousing stroke of his fingers, making her want him with an intensity that arched her body and made her head thrash wildly from side to side on the pillow.

'Elliott!' His name was torn from her throat on a sob of anguish, and, as though he knew what she was feeling, he lifted her hands from his shoulders and drew them the full length of his body.

'Bea, you don't know how much I've ached for this!'

She cried out beneath the fierce pressure of his kiss, and then gave herself up to it, stunned by the depth and intensity of his passion.

The feeling that he was holding something back, not giving all of himself to her, goaded her, making

her move provocatively against him, demanding
more than he was giving.

She felt him tense and then his eyes looked down
into hers, dark with strain and need and something
more primitive and dangerous.

'Bea, you're making it impossible for me to remember this is your first time.'

His voice shook and so did his body, the fierce
thrust of it within her own suddenly wildly out of
control. She clung to him, hearing him moan her
name, feeling the sudden quickening of her own
flesh as it responded to his male need.

Tiny quivers of sensation built up inside her, a
quivery, shivery tension that wouldn't let her go,
that drove her to incite him to take her with him to
that place where the boundaries of flesh and mor-
tality exploded in a vast shimmering ball of sensation.

The knowledge that someone was touching her
woke her. She opened her eyes and stretched, tensing as she felt her body's unfamiliar stiffness.

'It's getting late.'

Elliott was bending over her, fully dressed. Immediately she remembered what had happened. At
some point he had covered her with a quilt, she realised, grabbing hold of it and holding it protectively over her nudity.

Now that her mind was no longer dazed by sexual desire she was cringingly aware of all that she
had betrayed.

'You and I have a lot to talk about.'

She bit her lip, releasing it immediately when she realised how tender it was.

'I have to go to France on business for a few days, but once I get back . . .'

Those weren't the words she wanted to hear, Beatrice realised achingly. She wanted to be held in his arms and told that he loved her.

Sex wasn't the same for an experienced man in his mid-thirties as it was for a twenty-seven-year-old virgin, she reflected miserably. She didn't need to tell Elliott how she felt. The very fact that they had made love at all had said it all.

How could she have not known that she loved him? How could she have been stupid enough not to see what lay behind her own antipathy towards him? Or had she been stupid? Hadn't that antipathy been an excellent form of camouflage, a marvellous protective wall to hide behind? Now she had no camouflage, no wall. She was exposed and vulnerable . . . too vulnerable . . .

'Bea . . .'

She felt the bed depress as Elliott sat down. His hand cupped her face, but she jerked away.

She couldn't bear to hear him say that it had all been a mistake, that he had given in to the impulse of the moment and now regretted it. That telling her he loved her had meant nothing and that she should forget all about it.

'I'd like to get dressed.'

She deliberately made her voice sound cold. Inside she was a mass of seething, rioting emotions, but she didn't want to hear whatever it was Elliott wanted to talk to her about because she was sure she wasn't going to like it. She had fallen for one of the oldest tricks in the book; she deserved the pain she was suffering now for being stupid enough to believe that a man like Elliott could love her. The fact that she had believed it showed how desperate for his love she had been.

'Bea...'

'We must get back. Everyone will be wondering where on earth we are.'

Mortification filled her, but she stubbornly refused to listen to the anger she could sense hardening his voice.

'Stop being such a little fool! We can't change what's happened.' He sounded absolutely furious.

Beatrice felt her face go red. She wanted to scream at him that it was his fault. He had been the one to arouse her to the point where she forgot... Where she forgot that she was plain and dull, she told herself bitterly. Oh yes, Elliott was quite a magician; he had certainly worked some sort of spell on her, but it was over now. She couldn't pretend to understand why he had wanted to make love to her. It couldn't be because he loved her, no matter what he might have said. And that had been before... No such words of love had fallen from his lips after they had made love, had they?

'Bea...'

'I don't want to talk about it, Elliott. Please go away and let me get dressed.'

She heard him swear as he got off the bed, but she didn't move until she heard the door close behind him.

It was a silent drive back to Wimbledon. Beatrice knew she was very quiet during supper, but as usual none of her family appeared to notice that there was anything wrong. At least she was spared the humiliation of anyone else knowing what had happened, she told herself.

How many other foolish women had Elliott seduced at the house by using that same ploy? she tormented herself after supper was over.

She was relieved when Elliott announced that he had to go out. She didn't think she could have endured to be in the same room with him for much longer. She heard him saying something to Henrietta about his trip to France. How *could* she go on living under the same roof with him now?

Her thoughts swirled round and round, tormenting her, past insecurities rising to taunt her, all that she had felt in Elliott's arms forgotten as she gave in to the insidious tug of her old insecurity complex.

Elliott couldn't possible love anyone like her; thus it followed that he had simply been amusing himself with her. She had been fool enough to fall for it, and that was an end to the matter.

CHAPTER EIGHT

'WHERE did Elliott take you for lunch the other day? You never did tell us.'

Beatrice and Ben were alone in the small sitting-room. Beatrice was sewing buttons on the boys' shirts and Benedict had wandered in.

She felt her skin flush as she instinctively bent protectively over her sewing.

'Oh, he wanted to show me a house he's bought.'

She saw Benedict frown.

'What on earth for? You've fallen for him, haven't you?' he demanded, stunning her with his perception. 'I knew this would happen! Bea, don't let him hurt you. Oh, he's a smooth bastard, I'll grant you that, but he's just playing with you. I mean, you've only got to look at the women he's been out with.' He put his arm round her shoulder and tilted her face up to his with his other hand.

'Oh, God, he's already hurt you, hasn't he?'

She couldn't stop the tears from welling and then spilling down over her cheeks.

'Oh, Bea, why did you let him do it? You must have known you were out of your league. You've seen the sort of women he dates. God, Bea, why did you let him get to you? You know how he feels about us as a family. I suppose he picked on you because he knows you're the most vulnerable. But I never thought you'd fall for something like that.'

Ben shook his head sadly, watching her out of the corner of his eye.

Beatrice was too overwhelmed by her own feelings to look at him properly or to observe the slightly calculating expression hardening his eyes.

Ben was right, why on earth hadn't she realised the truth for herself? After all, she had noticed often enough how Elliott would stand and watch her family with supercilious amusement. She had known how he seemed at times almost to dislike them. Of course he would be amused by how easily he could get at them through her.

Round and round her agitated thoughts swirled, stirring up such muddy water that she no longer knew what was real and what wasn't. Ben was right about one thing, though: she was a fool...a fool for thinking that Elliott might actually love her.

As though in confirmation of her thoughts, Ben added softly, 'Bea, how could you let him make a fool of you like that? I mean, it's not as though... Well, you're just not his type, are you? You must have realised that... You must have wondered why...' He broke off in patent embarrassment, allowing the full force of his words to take effect.

Pain ran through her like red-hot wires as she was forced to confront reality and see herself as others saw her. The image Ben had just held up to her was not a flattering one... But it was the real one, she thought miserably, and he was right. Of course Elliott could never really have been interested in a woman like her.

'Of course, it's different here in the family,' Ben went on comfortingly. 'We know and appreciate you for what you really are, but Elliott... He hasn't gone to France on his own, you know,' he told her quietly. 'Look at this.'

He unfolded the newspaper he was holding, and opened it at the gossip page. Beatrice felt the pain inside her tighten its wrenching claws as she made out the grainy picture of Elliott, a tall blonde woman clinging possessively to his side.

'That's Maria Stephens, the actress,' Ben told her unnecessarily.

The phone rang and he went to answer it. Resolutely Beatrice refused to look again at the photograph. Ben was right, she had been a complete and utter fool.

Suddenly she longed to get away... from her family, her home... from everything. She ached to escape, to be alone...

Ben came back in.

'I'm sorry, I've to go out.' He hesitated awkwardly. 'You'll... you'll be OK, won't you?'

It was as much as she could manage to nod her head.

'I... I won't tell the others anything about this.'

She bit down hard on her lip, ignoring the pain inflicted by her teeth.

She heard the front door slam. She was alone. Henrietta was out shopping and she had the house to herself. And she ought to be on her way to work. She was going in later that morning because Jon wanted her to work later that evening.

Work was the last thing she felt like, but at least it might take her mind off her problems. How could Elliott have done this to her? No, she corrected her-

self bitterly, how could she have done it to herself?
She had believed him because she wanted to believe
him . . . a pathetic apology for a real woman, a sex-
starved virgin who had wanted him too badly to
question her motives. It wasn't a pleasant picture,
but bravely she faced up to it. It was better than admitting the real truth—that she loved him and
probably had done for years without realising it.
Elliott had realised it, though. He must have done
to be sure she would be vulnerable to his lies. That
made her writhe in an agony of self-abasement that
took her as far as the front door and her car.

She really wasn't fit to drive, she admitted to
herself as she pulled up in front of Jon's house. In
her present state it was a miracle that she hadn't had
an accident.

She opened the heavy Victorian front door with
the key that Jon had given her and made her way to
the music room. For once, no sound reached her
from within it.

As she opened the door, she blinked to make sure
she wasn't seeing things as she surveyed the extraordinary chaos within the room. Jon was standing
by his piano rifling frantically through a pile of
music. He didn't look up until she had called his
name three times.

'Bea, thank God you've arrived! The Florence
contract has been brought forward and I've got to
fly out there in two days' time. I'm never going to
be ready in time!'

Somehow she managed to convince him that the
lost score would be found much faster if he sat
down and she did the looking.

It took her less than twenty minutes to discover it underneath a pile of discarded magazines.

'How on earth am I going to manage in Florence without you?' Jon fretted as he thanked her. 'You've got to come with me. We can fix you up with a ticket and sort out some accommodation...' His eyes brightened as he warmed to the idea. 'I need you, Bea. I can't imagine how on earth I ever managed without you.'

Florence... She would be safely out of Elliott's reach, safely away from the torment of anyone else realising what had happened. She would be...safe.

The thought beckoned and lured her on all morning, one half of her saying that it was both impossible and irresponsible that she should go, the other yearning so strongly for the solitude and protection the thought offered that she had to stop herself from agreeing to Jon's suggestion immediately.

Florence—escape. Both words echoed through her thoughts all day, and in the end she compromised by telling Jon that provided his agent could make suitable arrangements for her travel and lodging she would go with him.

She could hardly believe she had behaved so impulsively, and part of her mind hoped in a way that his agent wouldn't be able to make the arrangements, but it seemed that fate was against her. Not only could he make them but he was overwhelmed with joy and relief that she was going.

'Jon needs someone to organise him,' he told her over the phone. He had been scared to death that the young composer would leave some vital piece of paper on the plane, or worse still forget to actually get on it. Now he could sleep easily, knowing that Jon was in Beatrice's capable hands.

She didn't say a word at home. After all, she was escaping, and prisoners did not normally give advance warning of their intent.

Prisoners. She tested the word, surprised by her instinctive mental use of it. Was that really how she saw herself, as a prisoner? Of whom?

Not her family, surely?

Well, perhaps her own guilt at her need to escape from them, she told herself, unwilling to admit the truth. There were times when she longed to escape from her responsibilities, to be free to be herself. And now that need was intensified by the greater desire to get away from Elliott. How on earth could she ever face him again?

She would need her summer clothes for Florence. She looked at them as she laid them on her bed, suddenly irritated by the dullness of them, but they were all she had.

Elliott rang the evening before her departure. Ben answered the phone, and when he told her who was on the line, she shook her head and told him to tell Elliott she was out. She had no idea why he wanted to talk to her, unless it was to tell her that he was bringing his blonde companion back with him.

She was stunned by how much the thought of him with someone else hurt, and by the fact that she had lived so many adult years without being aware of her capacity for such pain. She felt rather like a small animal, used to the cover and darkness of night, suddenly exposed to the harshness of full sunlight—and it hurt.

The flight to Pisa left Heathrow late in the morning. Her case was packed, her taxi was picking Jon up on the way to the airport.

Before she left, she sat down and wrote a note to Henrietta telling her that she was going away for a few days.

After destroying three attempts to explain just why this had been necessary, she was half-way through the fourth when the taxi arrived. Hastily signing it, she sealed the envelope and dropped it on the kitchen table.

It was only when the taxi actually pulled out of the drive that she realised she was holding her breath, as though in fear of one of her family suddenly appearing to stop her from leaving.

The flight to Pisa was relatively uneventful, apart from Jon having to be reassured several times that they had not left any vital piece of paper behind them in London.

They were met at the airport by an expensive chauffeur-driven car which drove them on to Florence where they were taken to an equally expensive but slightly crumbling hotel that echoed the mediaeval overtones that haunted the city as it basked in the hot summer sun.

Jon had a suite, complete with piano, and Beatrice waited to see him comfortably settled in it before asking to be taken to her own room.

It was off the same corridor, several doors down, a large high-ceilinged room with ornate plasterwork and a huge bed. She had no private sitting-room, but her bedroom was equipped with a desk and more than adequate cupboard space. She also had a cavernous bathroom, with a bath with clawed feet and a rather odd-looking lion's head instead of taps.

Unpacking didn't take her very long. Jon hadn't eaten on the plane and she ordered them both sandwiches and coffee.

He wasn't due to meet the director of the opera company until the evening. Both of them had been invited to have dinner at the director's home, and as she surveyed the meagre contents of her wardrobe, Beatrice acknowledged that she had nothing very elegant to wear.

Before they had left England, Jon's agent, who had seen them off at the airport, had pushed into her hand what seemed like an enormous quantity of lire, telling her gruffly when she tried to refuse them, 'Expenses. They live a pretty sophisticated life out there, and since you're babysitting Jon, you'll need clothes to fit the part. Jon needs a new dinner-suit as well.'

The money was already burning a hole in her pocket, and she recognised with a faint start how long it was since she had had both the money and the leisure time to shop exclusively for herself.

She and Jon had their sandwiches and their coffee. She ordered a taxi to take them to the Fioris', and as she went back to her own room to prepare for the evening she realised that so far she had not given a single thought to her family.

Elliott, though, was a different matter. There had not been so much as a single second when he had been out of her thoughts.

Since her only evening dress was her black velvet, she was forced to wear it, and as she and Jon descended to the very grand foyer of the hotel to wait for their taxi, she couldn't help noticing how shabbily their clothes contrasted with the elegantly dressed people thronging the entrance to the hotel. All of them were unmistakably Italian, apart from a smattering of Americans of a type far removed from the caricature tourist one normally associated with that country—women in Bill Blass and Alfonso, men in expensive suits—but even they could not match their Italian counterparts. The dinner-suit must have been invented with the Italian male in mind, thought Beatrice, watching them, and as for their female companions... She searched for an adjective to adequately describe their aura of polished chic and admitted herself defeated. It wasn't just their clothes, or their immaculately made-up faces and styled hair. It was their assurance, their innate belief in their own femininity. Not one of them wore anything even remotely identifiable with a pair of trousers, and not one of them looked as though she were not completely and absolutely in control of her own life. No careworn, dutiful, oppressed wives, these!

She felt relieved when their taxi eventually arrived. People had been staring at them, tactfully of course, but she couldn't help but be aware of how out of place they must look: she in her shabby worn velvet, Jon in a dinner-suit that looked as though it had been bought for someone else.

He explained to her that he had bought it off the peg, without trying it on, and that he had got mixed up about his size.

The Fioris lived in an impressive Palladian villa outside the city. Beatrice caught tantalising glimpses of its honey-yellow plasterwork as their taxi climbed through the cypress-shadowed darkness towards it.

Floodlighting illuminated the formal Italian gardens. The house looked as though it genuinely might be eighteenth-century, and Beatrice wondered if it possessed one of the marvellously intricate water gardens the Italians of that period had been so fond of.

The moment their taxi drew to a halt, the imposing front door opened. However, it was not an immaculately clad butler who greeted them, as she had half expected, but their host and hostess.

Carlo Fiori was tall for an Italian and very distinguished-looking, his dark hair shading to silver grey at his temples. Tall and athletic, he possessed the classic features beloved of the Graeco-Roman sculptors. His wife was also tall, her figure built on almost Junoesque lines, Beatrice realised, almost gasping with admiration as she saw how Lucia Fiori had emphasised rather than concealed the full curves of her body, clothing them in rich, almost stingingly brilliant coloured silks that set off her olive skin and dark hair.

A single diamond, brilliantly cut, glittered against her wedding ring as she extended her hands in a warm welcome. Her nails were long and varnished, their elegance making Beatrice immediately long to hid her own short, work-roughened paws behind her back.

'So, at last we get to meet,' Carlo Fiori greeted Jon, shaking hands exuberantly with him, apparently unaware of the almost ludicrous fit of Jon's dinner-suit.

Lucia was equally welcoming to Beatrice, ushering her inside out of what she described as a 'cool evening breeze'. In point of fact, to Beatrice, in her heavy velvet, the atmosphere was really too warm.

Having seen the elegance of the Fioris' home and appearance, she was more relieved than ever that the four of them would be dining alone.

Lucia led them all to a conservatory at the back of the house, filled with greenery. In the background Beatrice could hear the musical sound of cascading water. They were dining intimately round a small round table, but despite their informal surroundings their meal was impeccably chosen and served by highly trained staff, and while she ate Beatrice was able to observe the almost maternal care that Lucia exhibited towards her husband.

She was a woman well used to dealing with erratic genius, Beatrice recognised, and one who obviously good-temperedly knew that there were times when her importance in her husband's life took second place to his music.

'Carlo is a very gifted musical director,' she told Beatrice later over coffee while the two men went to Carlo's music room to discuss the opera. 'I understand this. One must make allowances for genius. I sense that you understand this too.' She looked speculatively at Beatrice and asked quite openly, 'Forgive me if I trespass, but are you and Jon...'

Immediately Beatrice shook her head. 'No, there's nothing like that.'

'Ah, I thought from the way you accompanied him at the last moment...'

'I wanted to escape.'

The admission surprised her. She never normally confided in anyone, and yet somehow without her being aware how it had happened Lucia had eased the truth out of her.

'From a man? Forgive me if I intrude, but sometimes it is good to talk about these things. Carlo sometimes bottles things up and then pff! We have an explosion.' Lucia made an expansive gesture with her hands that made Beatrice laugh.

'From a man,' she agreed unsteadily, 'and from my family,'

'Ah, you have a family. They do not treat you very well, this family, if you have to run away from them. Why is that, I wonder?'

'Because I've let them treat me like a doormat.'

Again the admission startled Beatrice. Why had she never admitted this to herself before? Why had she put up with her family's selfishness if she had secretly resented it? Elliott had been right, she *had* been a martyr. She flinched almost physically away from the thought of him.

'You must tell me more about this family of yours,' Lucia encouraged. 'I too have a family. They did not want me to marry Carlo...they did not approve of the artistic temperament; they are industrialists from Milano. But I fell in love...' She shrugged and smiled. 'But first I want to know more about this man you have had to escape from.'

Beatrice reflected how extraordinary it was that she didn't resent Lucia's open curiosity. On the contrary, it was almost a relief to unburden herself to her and to talk about everything that had happened.

Once she had started, the words simply seemed to pour out of her—surely in too confused a jumble to be understood, but Lucia seemed to know instinctively what she was trying to say.

'So, he says he loves you, this man, and then pff, he is gone, and you begin to think as every woman in love has thought . . . does he love me, or is he deceiving me?

'That is something we can do nothing about. I do not know this man and therefore I cannot speak for his feelings, but the other . . . this ridiculous belief you have that you are a plain woman and therefore not fit to be loved . . . that we can put to rights.' Lucia laughed at Beatrice's bemused expression.

'This is Italy, where a woman knows that first of all she must believe in herself as a woman, and that comes from here . . .' She touched her chest. 'However, there are one or two tricks. I will teach them to you.'

'Oh, but I'm here to work for Jon,' protested Beatrice.

'He will be too busy working with my husband. I know Carlo, he is most impressed with your young friend. He will wish to spend many hours with him talking, arguing . . . He thrives on it. They will quarrel and Jon will say he wants to go home. You

will speak to him calmly and he will stay, but in between times you and I will discover why it is you do
not believe you are an attractive woman. In Italy,
you know, we like a woman to be shaped like a
woman.' Lucia's smile was mischievous. 'You will
see...'

Lucia Fiori was the age Beatrice's mother would
have been if she was still alive; she was beautiful and
elegant, as femininely attractive in her way as her
mother had been in hers, and yet in her company
Beatrice did not feel clumsy or ugly. Lucia had a
warmth that her mother had never had, she recognised sadly, a compassion for people that had never
touched her mother's life.

'It is of great sadness to me that Carlo and I have
never had children, and so when I find someone to
whom I am drawn I adopt them into my heart and
family.' Lucia saw Beatrice's start of surprise and
laughed. 'Ah yes, now I see what it is about you that
made this man so angry. You flinch back from
emotion and affection as though you are afraid it
will burn you. It is just as well that you have run
away from this selfish family of yours, but as for
this man... I think you will not run from him quite
so easily.'

How on earth Lucia could make such an assess-
ment on the scanty information she had given her,
Beatrice didn't know. What she did know was that
the very thought of Elliott taking the trouble to
track her down made her heart thump and her
pulses soar. But Lucia was wrong. Elliott wouldn't
try to find her. Why should he? To him she had
simply been a challenge, his seduction of her a

symbol of the contempt he felt for her whole family.

She couldn't believe it when the two men came to join them and she realised it was gone one o'clock. She felt an affinity towards Lucia that surprised her, and when the older woman announced in firm tones that she would pick her up at the hotel the next morning to show her the city, she did not demur.

On the way back in the taxi she discovered that Jon had been equally impressed by Carlo.

'Tomorrow he is to show me the Opera House and introduce me to his staff,' he told her.

'Then you won't mind if I spend the morning with Lucia?'

He looked surprised that she needed to ask him. She was here under false pretences, she thought a little guiltily. Jon didn't really need her.

But the next morning she managed to assuage some of her guilt when she discovered that Jon had apparently misplaced his precious score. He was as irritable as a small child on the verge of a temper tantrum, refusing all her attempts to soothe him.

'You had the score when we arrived,' she reminded him. 'It can't have disappeared.'

'The maids must have taken it. I knew I should have made a copy. I . . .'

He had thrown the jacket to his dinner-suit on to a chair, and as Beatrice automatically picked it up she discovered the missing papers lying underneath it. As she handed them to him he scowled horribly, and she had to suppress a small laugh.

'Come on now and have some breakfast,' she coaxed. Unlike her own family who never needed to be encouraged to eat, Jon was prone to ignoring mealtimes, and she had to virtually stand over him while he consumed some grapefruit and a slice of wholemeal toast.

If he ever married, his wife would need to be a combination of maid and mother, she thought wryly when he had finally gathered everything together and was ready to leave.

They went down to the foyer together. Beatrice was wearing a linen suit she had had for years. It was navy and did little for her colouring, and she felt excruciatingly conscious of that fact the moment she stepped into the foyer. What was it about Florence that was making her so aware of the limitations of her wardrobe? At home she had barely given her clothes a thought. Perhaps it was the sight of so many frankly curvaceous bodies dressed in stunningly brilliant silks and linens.

At home she had never bothered because she had known that no matter what she wore she could never look like her slim-hipped, narrow-framed sisters and mother. All her life she had been programmed to think that their shape was the feminine ideal and that any deviation from it was to be abhorred.

Now in Florence she was discovering that there were women who were positively proud of their curvaceous shapes; that breasts and hips and tiny narrow waists were apparently assets to be flaunted rather than burdens to be discreetly hidden beneath loose layers of clothes.

'First we shall have a *cappuccino*, and then, we go shopping,' announced Lucia when the two men had

left. She summoned a waiter who escorted them to
the very smart coffee lounge, already three-quarters
full of elegant women, some with equally immaculately dressed dark-eyed and dark-haired children.

Elliott's child would look a little like that,
Beatrice found herself thinking as she studied one
tough-looking little boy with wicked dark eyes and
a watermelon grin. She caught back the thought,
suppressing the wave of pain that accompanied it.
What if she was pregnant? What if she was already
carrying Elliott's child?

She knew such a prospect ought to fill her with
anxiety, but instead what she actually felt was a tiny
thrill of delight. Elliott's child... Unknowingly her
eyes became dreamy, and Lucia who was watching
her felt a tiny resurgence of her own pain. To bear
the child of the man whom one loved... She gave a
soft sigh, and reminded herself that her life was full
and busy, and that right now she had on her hands
just the sort of challenge she enjoyed the most.

They drank their coffee, rich and creamily
fragrant, and then Beatrice dutifully followed Lucia
outside and into a waiting taxi.

They were dropped off in a narrow street filled
with obviously exclusive shops, and Beatrice found
herself drooling over the bewildering display of
shoes and bags in one window. Shoes in every
colour of the rainbow and then some more... Shoes
with high heels and narrow straps... Shoes de-
signed to emphasise the femininity of their wear-
ers... Shoes that were totally impractical and
instantly desirable.

'We start from underneath and then work out,' Lucia told her firmly, coaxing her away.

If this was the sort of underwear commonly worn by Italian women, it was no wonder their men looked so happy, Beatrice reflected bemusedly half an hour later, surveying the mass of silks, cottons and lace tumbled over the counter of the exclusive boutique they were in.

At home the full curves of her breasts had meant that bras tended to be functional rather than ornamental, but here... The delicious profusion of pastel lingerie made her mouth water. She touched the garments longingly, and, as though sensing her weakness, Lucia encouraged, 'A woman needs to feel silk against her skin. It makes her feel all the more conscious of the difference when it is a man's body that caresses her flesh.'

She delivered the comment so openly and matter-of-factly that Beatrice could do little more than blink. The hot blush that covered her ten seconds later was born of her own very private memories of what it had been like to feel Elliott's hands and flesh against her own, and had nothing to do with any embarrassment over Lucia's calm comment.

Because she had grown up to think of her body as ugly, something to be ashamed of rather than proud, she had never even thought of adorning it with such feminine self-indulgences as expensive underwear; now she was discovering, just as she had discovered with Mirry's camiknickers, that she could wear delicate silks and satins and look good in them.

The assistant marvelled over her tiny waist and narrow ribcage, and somehow or other she found herself buying two sets of outrageously expensive underwear. She had to use her credit card to pay for it, stalwartly having refused to use her lire. She knew that Jon's agent said she was to be appropriately dressed, but somehow she didn't think satin underwear was what he had in mind.

'Now we will find you something to wear over them,' Lucia promised as they left the small boutique. 'In here, I think.'

'In here' was a narrow doorway with a single, very small window with one garment displayed in it. Once inside, they had to go up a narrow flight of stairs into the shop itself.

The assistant who glided forward to meet them was almost as curvaceous as Lucia, although much younger. Lucia spoke quickly to her in Italian and she disappeared, reappearing several minutes later to escort both women into a luxuriously equipped fitting-room in which were already hanging several garments in rich colours of saffron yellow and burnished topaz, a brilliant cobalt blue and lime, and even a hint of deep rich pink; colours chosen to complement her chestnut colouring.

If she had once thought that such rich and vibrant colours could never be for her, now Beatrice discovered that she was wrong.

An exquisitely cut linen suit in a natural colour, teamed with a saffron silk blouse, transformed her instantly into a sophisticated woman of style and verve. The expertly cut skirt skimmed her waist and curved over her hips ending just on her knees. There

was a small split up the back seam and three buttons, only one of which was fastened. The jacket
was unstructured and yet smart, and the assistant
showed her how to roll back the sleeves and fold the
saffron silk of her blouse sleeves over the top of
them.

She tried on so many outfits that she finally lost
count of them, but Lucia had no such problems.

'The linen suit and the saffron blouse,' she pronounced when Beatrice was once again dressed in
her own clothes, 'and I think the saffron linen dress
for day wear. It looked extremely chic.'

She also suggested a softly drop-waisted dress in
subtle blending shades of peach and coffee which
Beatrice herself had fallen for.

'It will do for informal lunches and dinners; and
of course for evening you must have the peach silk.'

The dress in question was in actual fact a two-
piece in a heavy silk satin and cut in such a way that
it draped across one shoulder, completely exposing
the other, the slanting line echoed in the hem of the
tunic top and then again in the hem of the skirt, so
that at one side the skirt exposed the entire length of
her leg from mid-thigh down and, at the other, it
demurely skimmed mid-calf.

The satin was softly pleated so that it fell softly,
moving as she moved. It made her skin glow and her
body take on a veiled allure that made her stare at
herself with bewildered rounded eyes.

A silk two-piece in brilliant jade was added to the
growing pile, and then, to Beatrice's consternation
and before she could protest, Lucia announced that
she was going to pay for their purchases.

'No, I insist. It is a great treat for me to have an adoptive daughter to spoil. I am enjoying myself!'

Beatrice didn't doubt that, but her thrifty soul was shocked by the expenditure of so many lire.

'Shoes,' pronounced Lucia, 'and then I think we shall call it a day. Tomorrow I shall take you to the salon where I have my hair done. Yours is lovely, but such an old-fashioned heavy style. It does nothing for your lovely bone structure.'

Beatrice felt her heart tighten swiftly in pain. Elliott had told her she had good bone structure, and she had melted beneath his praise, mindlessly giving herself up to him, wanting to believe him so much that she had not even questioned...

'Are you all right?'

Lucia's hand on her arm reminded her of where she was. She gave her hostess a small empty smile and followed her out of the shop.

By the time they reached the shoe shop she had herself partially under control. This time she insisted on paying for her own purchases, trying not to feel too ludicrously flattered by the assistant's praise of her small feet and delicate ankles.

Once again she and Jon had dinner with the Fioris, and Beatrice was too tired to protest when Lucia reminded her that she would be calling for her again in the morning.

CHAPTER NINE

'THERE'S something different about you.'

Jon frowned as Beatrice tied the bow tie of the dinner-suit she had bullied him into buying.

Tonight they were dining formally with the Fioris at a dinner party given to introduce Jon to their friends.

'It's my hair,' she told him self-consciously. Even now she was not used to the shock of her new appearance.

Lucia's stylist had cut her hair to shoulder length in a blunt bob that showed off its colour and curl. He had blown it softly into a style that seemed to make her eyes look enormous and her cheekbones very high. It was the sort of style she had seen in fashion magazines and had never thought suitable for herself.

'I like it. And your eyes look different as well.'

The beautician at the salon had shown her several new ways of applying her make-up, so that it looked both natural and effective.

Tonight she was wearing the peach evening two-piece, and every time she caught a glimpse of herself in a mirror she was bemused by her own reflection. She looked so different, so...so sophisticated and attractive, she decided on a sudden spurt of defiance. Under Lucia's tutelage she was learning to believe that a woman did not have to be tall and reed-slender to be physically attractive, and as she and Jon went downstairs to the foyer, the admiring looks she received confirmed that Lucia had been right.

One man walking past her even leaned towards her to murmur caressingly, '*Bella . . . bella . . .*' and she had to blink away the sudden film of tears blinding her as she tried to fight down the memory of Elliott calling her 'Bella Bea'. Only he had not meant it, had he?

The other guests at the dinner party were all Italian and all connected with the operatic world, but Beatrice found herself far from bored. For a start her dinner partner was a very romantic-looking young tenor, who scarcely took his eyes off her all through the meal; very heady stuff for a young woman used to thinking of herself as unattractive to the male sex, and Riccardo was certainly just as handsome as any of the male actors that Lucilla brought home.

She had enough experience of her parents' dinner parties to be discreetly flattering when necessary, judging that operatic egos were probably no less in need of the odd adulatory massage than thespian ones.

After dinner she learned from Jon that progress on the new opera was going well, and that he and Carlo found themselves in excellent accord, and all in all by the end of the evening Beatrice felt as though she had come a long way from the woman who had stood in her bedroom and wept over her brother's unthinking reinforcement of her own view that she lacked any of the feminine assets necessary to keep Elliott by her side.

She wasn't completely deluding herself, though, she reflected as she and Jon were driven back to their hotel by Carlo. She might, through Lucia's kindness, have come to appreciate her own worth as a woman, but that did not alter the way she felt about Elliott—nor his lack of feelings for her. As always when she thought about him she felt a deep ache begin inside her.

They had reached the hotel. Beatrice suppressed a yawn as Carlo helped her out of the car. It was almost two o'clock in the morning. What time would that make it at home? she wondered muzzily.

Tomorrow she really ought to telephone them and check that Henrietta was coping. Still, at least they would not be worrying about her; they knew from her note where she was and with whom. She struggled to suppress another yawn, and blushed guiltily as she saw Carlo watching her in amusement.

'I'm sorry, but I'm just not used to late nights,' she apologised.

'A situation which I suspect will be remedied before your visit is over,' Carlo teased.

He had not been blind to the attentions his young tenor had been paying Beatrice during dinner. 'Riccardo asked me where you were staying,' he told her.

'Carlo, I've just had a thought about the second act,' Jon interrupted. 'Do you have time to discuss it with me now?'

'But of course. I shall come up to your suite with you.'

Beatrice left the two men outside the door to Jon's suite. Her own bedroom was only a few yards down the corridor, but she liked the way that Carlo waited until she was safely inside before following Jon. There was no doubt about it, Italian men knew how to make a woman feel cherished.

Dreamily she removed her make-up and then brushed her hair, admiring the way it immediately curved back into its new style.

She had a leisurely bath, soaking in the rose-scented water and then patting herself dry with the luxuriously thick towels supplied by the hotel, before putting on the new nightdress that Lucia had secretly added to her lingerie purchases as a surprise present.

The nightdress was made in fine silk crêpe-de-chine in the softest apple green. Delicate straps supported the bodice which modestly just covered the upper curves of her breasts, but at the back it dipped right down to the base of her spine before falling to the floor. There was a bias-cut jacket that went with it, which also dipped to a point at the back, just low enough to cover the flesh exposed by the nightdress.

She had just finished moisturising her face when she heard a knock on her bedroom door. Frowning, she went to answer it.

'It is only me, Carlo,' she heard the Italian call softly to her through the door. 'Jon has some notes he would like you to type up for him first thing in the morning, on the amendments to the second act. May I come in?'

Beatrice opened and door and let him in.

There was nothing remotely sexual or intimidating about the smile Carlo gave her; indeed she might have been fully clothed for all the attention he paid to her silk-clad body, and once again she applauded the Italian male for his subtle ability to convey so much with just a single look. Carlo's look to her said that she was a very attractive young woman, whom he, a happily married older man, saw as adopted niece or goddaughter.

'These are Jon's notes,' he told her, producing several sheets of scribbled paper. 'I believe you have a portable typewriter with you?'

'Yes. I know Jon's appointment with you tomorrow isn't until eleven, so I shall have them ready for him in plenty of time.'

Beatrice was just about to make a comment on how great a fraud she felt in accompanying Jon, when she was silenced by a determined rap on her bedroom door.

Her first thought that it must be Jon was speedily despatched when she heard the unmistakable and decidedly harsh sound of Elliott's voice calling to her through the door.

'I know you're in there, Beatrice. Open this door!'

She was frozen to the spot, unable to comprehend that Elliott was actually outside, that he had actually followed her out here to Florence. Joy warred with apprehension, her face clearly betraying her thoughts as Carlo watched her in sympathetic understanding, inwardly reflecting that he was glad that he was no longer so young and vulnerable. All his energies were absorbed by running the opera company, and he was glad to be able to relax in the knowledge that Lucia was the loving and understanding partner that she was.

'I think you'd better let him in,' he said softly, 'because if you don't I suspect he will find his own method of entry.'

The thought of having to explain to the hotel how her door-lock came to be forced was enough to galvanise Beatrice into action.

A pretty flush warmed her skin as she hurried over and unlocked the door.

Elliott pushed past her and stormed in, leaving her to close the door behind him as he turned to face her. He looked hot and tired, she noticed, his suit jacket rumpled, and his skin bearing the tell-tale signs of exhaustion.

'Now perhaps you'd be kind enough to tell me just what the hell's going on.'

Whatever his reason for coming to find her, it wasn't love, Beatrice decided, flinching away from his anger, watching his eyes darken and the betraying white line of temper harden round his mouth.

'I thought that you at least had some sense,' Elliott went on, 'but no, it seems that you're as idiotic as the rest of your precious family!'

He was bellowing at her as though she had gone deaf, Beatrice realised furiously, her own anger rising to meet his. Did he honestly think he could seduce her, walk away from her, and then turn up here shouting in anger at her, without even telling her what it was she was supposed to have done wrong?

'Elliott . . .'

'No wonder you ran away! You just couldn't wait to tell them, could you? It was a pity you weren't there to see the results of your duplicity. One of these days Benedict is going to make a good actor; at the moment he appears to relish some of his roles

a little too much. I never thought you were a coward, Beatrice. All you had to do was tell me you
didn't want to see me again. There was really no
need to go to the theatrical lengths of running away
and getting your brother to tell me.'

Beatrice was completely at sea. She couldn't
comprehend what Elliott was saying to her, but that
didn't seem to matter. What did matter was that he
had stormed into her bedroom and was berating her
as though he hated the very sight of her.

As though in confirmation of her thoughts he
advanced on her with gritted teeth and said furiously, 'I'd like to take hold of you and . . .'

The effect on Elliott of the gentle sound of Carlo's discreet cough might have been quite entertain-
ing in other circumstances. He stopped speaking
and stared across at him as he stepped out of the
shadows, his eyes going from Beatrice's nightdress-
clad body to Carlo's calm smile and then narrowing.

For no reason at all Beatrice had a vivid mental
image of the blonde clinging so possessively to his
arm as he left Heathrow, and, on a sudden spurt of
inventiveness, worthy of any Bellaire, she ran to
Carlo's side, tucking her arm through his and
clinging to him in a way that she hoped left no
doubt in Elliott's mind that she had replaced him.

If he could discard her so quickly for another
woman—well, she could do the same!

Carlo, always the impeccable gentleman, played
up to her as calmly as though the whole thing had
been rehearsed, and without giving either her or
Elliott an opportunity to speak said firmly,
'*Signore*, you are upsetting a very beautiful lady,

and that I fear I cannot allow. Permit me to send for the manager to escort you to your room, since you are clearly mistaken in thinking yourself welcome in this one.' He turned to Beatrice, squeezing her arm gently. 'Now, *cara*, do not upset yourself. You know I hate to see those pretty eyes marred by tears. Come, you get into bed. I shall deal with...this gentleman.'

Beatrice dared one brief look at Elliott, then closed her eyes, wishing she had not. He was a man in the grip of a violent rage. She could see him almost visibly grinding his teeth, his face suffused with a dark tide of colour that threatened imminent loss of self-control, but he was also too intelligent not to understand what Carlo was saying, and so, with a curt, 'This isn't going to be the end of this,' he turned on his heel and left, slamming the door behind him.

For nearly a whole minute Beatrice couldn't speak, and then when she tried to she was shaking so much that her teeth chattered. Carlo discreetly led her over to a chair and pushed her gently into it.

'That, I take it, is the reason my wife is so concerned about you?' he asked mildly, and as she looked at him Beatrice realised exactly what she had done and she stared at him in appalled embarrassment.

Trying to find the words to apologise and explain was impossible, but fortunately Carlo seemed to need no explanation.

'I see it is true what they say about your colour of hair, *signorina*,' he said with a charming smile. 'However, I must also confess that there was a great degree of provocation. A man who cannot see when

a woman is deeply in love with him deserves to believe that he has been replaced in her affections,
no?' he chuckled, and added thoughtfully, 'However, I must warn you that he did not strike me as a
man who will take such a blow with fortitude, and
I doubt that he will be deceived for very long.'

Beatrice couldn't speak for her mortification. It
must be something about the Italian air that was
affecting her like this. She had never in her whole
life done anything so out of character, and all she
could do was to blame her Bellaire genes and men-
tally thank her lucky stars that Carlo was so understanding.

It took her a long, long time to get to sleep. She
typed up Jon's notes to restore a sense of calm and
then, once she had overcome her own shock and
shame, she started to recall what Elliott had said to
her.

Of course Ben would have told him that she
didn't want to see him again simply to protect her,
but why should that make him so angry? She would
have thought it would have been the ideal get-out
for him, a discreet ending to an interlude that
should never have begun . . . would never have begun if she hadn't been so foolish as to fall in love
with him.

Perhaps he was angry because Ben had spiked his
guns and denied him the pleasure of parading her
folly in front of them all. But no, that was too theatrical and out of character for Elliott. The mere
fact that he knew of her vulnerability would be sufficient for him. He was not a man who cared about
the opinions or views of others, and certainly not

the opinions or views of the Bellaire clan. So why was he so furious?

She hoped she would never have to know. Once he realised she had another lover, surely he would return home, absolved from his responsibility for her. Surely once he realised there was someone else in her life, he would be relieved that there were to be no emotional repercussions from their brief affair...

As a consequence of her anguished thoughts she overslept, and was woken from a hauntingly emotional dream, in which Elliott was begging her to forgive him, by Jon calling to her through her bedroom door.

She leapt out of bed feeling thoroughly disorientated, relieved that she had decided to type up his notes before going to bed, and calling to him that she would be ready in ten minutes.

When she eventually joined him he seemed rather tense and on edge, and it seemed that while she overslept there had been a change of plan.

'I am meeting Carlo at a villa he owns near the coast,' he told her. 'It is very secluded, and he says that we can discuss my alterations to the score there without being interrupted. He is sending a car and a driver to take us there. He will be here in half an hour.' He chewed on his bottom lip and added awkwardly, 'Oh, and you'd better pack a few things.'

He saw her start of surprise and informed her, 'We may have to stay a couple of days, depending on how the alterations go. He had changed his mind about my amendments to the second act. He doesn't like them, and there will be a considerable amount of work to do on them.'

Beatrice blinked. It seemed that an awful lot had been going on while she was sleeping, but she was too used to the vagaries of the artistic temperament to comment, and it also struck her that Lucia's hand might be behind this move to get her away from Florence. Tucked away in the Fioris' villa, there would be little chance of Elliott catching up with her. Not that she felt he would try to after last night's débâcle. Even now she felt her skin flame with embarrassment when she remembered what she had done. How could she? Why on earth hadn't she simply faced up to Elliott and told him quietly that she knew that he had deceived her? Why all the histrionics? Deep down inside she knew why... pride. She hadn't wanted him to know that she had believed in him, that he had hurt her...

Her suspicion that Lucia had had a hand in events was reinforced when a maid appeared and announced that she had come to pack a case for her. Jon had ordered her some breakfast in his suite, and she went with him, having made sure that the maid knew to pack her portable typewriter.

Jon's tension was something she could understand in view of Carlo's change of heart about the second act of the opera, so she set herself the task of calming him down and reassuring him as she drank her coffee and ate fresh fruit and a croissant.

At eleven o'clock the telephone rang to announce that their car had arrived.

Jon carried their cases downstairs, handed them over to the uniformed chauffeur, then climbed into the back of the car with her.

The journey was a long one, almost two hours, the countryside they passed through mainly agricultural and empty of habitation.

At last Beatrice saw the glimmer of water in the distance and realised that they must be nearing their destination.

The villa was long and low and surrounded by well tended vines, although there was no one inside when the car stopped outside it. The chauffeur got out and removed their cases; Jon and Beatrice followed.

It was hotter here than in Florence, and Beatrice was glad to get inside. Her high heels rang loudly on the *terrazzo* tiles of the hallway as she followed the chauffeur up the stairs.

He stopped outside one of the bedroom doors and then pushed it open, gesturing to Beatrice to precede him.

She was in a pleasantly sized bedroom with a view over the back of the villa and the distant sea. She could smell herbs and dried lavender, and in the furnishing of the room she recognised Lucia's clever hand.

Here there was none of the expensive elegance of the Florence villa. Bare floorboards gleamed under a patina of wax, built up over many generations. Cool muslin draperies floated at the open window. The furniture was cherrywood and very traditional: the large bed had a polished wooden frame with head and tail boards and was matched by a solid wardrobe and a large chest of drawers with a mirror.

A rocking-chair with a quilted cover in the same pastel cottons as the comforter on the bed moved gently in the same breeze that wafted the curtains. This was a room that was redolent of the rich pageantry of life, Beatrice reflected. Generations had been born and had died in this room; she knew it without knowing why she had the knowledge. Joy and pain mingled with the elusive fragrance of lavender, tears and laughter.

The chauffeur had gone, presumably to take Jon's case to his room. In the distance she heard a car coming down the narrow track that led to the villa and knew it must be Carlo. Jon had already told her that Carlo had an appointment which prevented him from travelling with them.

She knew that, in addition to his chauffeur-driven Mercedes, Carlo possessed a fire-bright red Ferrari that Lucia claimed was the real love of his life, and no doubt in this monster he had made far better time than their leisurely progress.

She heard a car door slam and knew that she ought to go down and join the two men. After all, she was here to work, but she felt reluctant to leave the room: to face anyone, she admitted wryly.

A car engine fired and she presumed it was the chauffeur leaving for Florence. Everything was so quiet. She could hear birds singing.

There were footsteps on the stairs, their intrusion reminding her of how long she had been up there. She wasn't there to daydream but to work, and yet still there was this reluctance to move.

The door swung open, and her pulses leapt in sudden shocked recognition.

'Elliott!' she gasped.

'Beatrice!' he mocked, mimicking her shocked tone.

CHAPTER TEN

BEATRICE couldn't understand what was happening. She looked towards the door, expecting to see either Jon or Carlo behind him, but the house felt eerily empty of anyone other than themselves.

'Where... Where's Carlo?' she queried.

Elliott still looked tired, but not quite as drawn as he had looked last night.

This morning he was wearing clothes more appropriate to the climate: soft butter-yellow jeans and a matching short-sleeved shirt.

'You mean your lover.'

She could have sworn he was laughing at her behind the coolness of his unsmiling face. Her heart was tripping double time. She felt a swift stab of panic, a fear that something was wrong. She moistened her dry lips with the tip of her tongue, her stomach plunging sickly as she caught the look on Elliott's face.

It was such an intense combination of desire and pain that she couldn't believe it was directed at her.

'Why didn't you let anyone know where you were going?'

The question caught her off guard and she stared at him, not knowing what he was asking.

'I left a note...' she began.

'Yes, if you can call a few scribbled lines saying that you had to get away that. The whole house was in an uproar when I got back from France. For the first time in their spoiled, protected lives, the members of your family are aware of how much they depend on you.

'I know why you ran away, Beatrice, but I thought you had more sense than to pay any attention to Ben's fabrications. You must have realised that he...'

She didn't want to talk about how much he had hurt her; she dared not take the risk of breaking down completely in front of him.

'What are you doing here? Carlo...'

'You mean your lover.'

Again that secret note of amusement in his voice. She tossed her head and glared at him.

'It's no business of yours if I choose to take another lover!'

He stared hard at her, the amusement suddenly gone and a frightening grimness taking its place.

'If you genuinely believe that, then it's no wonder that Ben...' He broke off and came towards her until she was backing away from him. The windowsill jarred her back and she realised she had nowhere else to go.

'Did you really think the thought of you giving yourself to another man would stop me? Last night you'd have been well advised to get down on your knees and pray to God that what you told me wasn't true, but there wasn't any need for that, was there, Bea?'

She couldn't look at him. He was suffocatingly close to her; she could almost feel the heat coming off his body, and a rebellious part of her ached to reach out and touch him.

'I know everything, Bea, so it's no use continuing with this farce that Carlo is your lover. While you were lying asleep this morning I was talking to Lucia. I found her most informative.'

Beatrice felt the blood leave her face. How much had Lucia told him? Although she had never mentioned him by name, she knew that Lucia wouldn't have had much difficulty in realising who he was, and yet she couldn't believe that her friend had completely betrayed her.

'Your Carlo is a very fair-minded gentleman, I'll say that for him. Last night he helped you; today he's helped me.'

'I don't have anything to say to you, Elliott, so...'

'Then you're going to have to think of something, otherwise the next three days are going to be full of a lot of empty silences.'

Beatrice stared at him in disbelief.

'The next three days?' An awful feeling of realisation began to creep over her.

She pushed past him and ran across the landing to the window so that she could see the front of the villa.

It wasn't Carlo's Ferrari that stood outside, but an unfamiliar Mercedes coupé.

'It was all that I could hire this morning,' Elliott told her casually. 'There's no escape, Beatrice, you might as well resign yourself to it. You and I shall be spending the next three days here—alone. There's no phone, and no way out. You don't have an international driver's licence or any insurance, and the Italian police have some pretty stiff punishments for tourists driving under those circumstances.'

'But why? Why?' She whirled round and stared up at him, unable to comprehend why he had gone to such lengths to be alone with her, and how he had managed to persuade Lucia and Carlo to lend their aid.

'Do you really need to ask me that?' He leaned towards the wall, palms flat against it, entrapping her within the circle of his arms. Panic and need raced through her.

'Why are you *doing* this?' she demanded achingly. 'Haven't you had enough . . .'

'Pleasure out of tormenting me', she had been about to say, but he cut her off ruthlessly, his voice harsh and unfamiliar as he said thickly, 'Enough of you? Never!'

And she couldn't say any more because his head was bending towards her and she knew he was going to kiss her, and she couldn't do a damned thing about it other than to stand there quivering in mute anticipation.

'Beatrice, Beatrice, why did you run from me? You've just knocked ten years off my life, do you know that?'

The words were punctuated with soft kisses that teased her lips until they parted and clung to his, seeking more than such a brief tormenting touch.

'Ah, so you do want me!'

She tried to deny it, but the words remained locked in her throat, and anyway they would have been lies, as her response was very quickly proving to him.

He kissed her as though he was starving for her, no gentleness or restraint in the passionate onslaught of his mouth.

This time he was not coming to her as a prospective lover but as a man with an established right to a specific place in her life and in her arms, Beatrice recognised dizzily. There was possessiveness as well as need in the rough pressure of his mouth on hers, punishment, and the betrayal of a pain she had never expected him to disclose.

'How dare you run from me?' he demanded rawly, lifting his mouth a breath away from hers. 'How dare you frighten me half to death like that?'

His arms weren't braced against the wall any more, and his hands were running over her arms and then down her back and over her hips with fierce demanding movements that said quite plainly that he considered her his.

'Surely you knew what Ben was trying to do? Surely you knew, after what we'd shared, how I feel about you?'

He might as well have been talking in a foreign language, and her eyes told him as much.

'Dear God, Bea,' he groaned against her mouth. 'You can't have believed him. You *can't* have thought I'd go from your arms to another woman!'

She felt the fierceness in his body and tensed against it.

'Was that why you ran away? Because of me?'

She couldn't help it, she could feel tears pricking her eyes and then rolling betrayingly down her face.

She heard Elliott swear, and then her head was pushed gently into the curve of his shoulder, and his tongue was moving tenderly over her face, lapping up the salt tears.

'I never meant to hurt you. I thought you knew how I felt. I told you . . .'

'Ben said you were just playing with me... amusing yourself.' Her voice was rusty with pain.

'And you believed him? Beatrice, Beatrice, are you completely blind?'

'But why should Ben lie?'

She heard Elliott sigh as he lifted her head from its comfortable resting place and looked into her eyes.

'We'll deal with that one later; for now I've got more important things on my mind.'

'Such as?'

His eyes darkened, crinkling at the corners with amusement at the breathless note in her voice.

'Such as convincing a certain woman that I love her.'

He picked her up as easily as though she weighed no more than Mirry, and placed her down on the bed.

'I've wanted you so much. I couldn't believe it when I got back and found you gone.' His voice shook, and she looked up at him in bemusement, seeing the faint sheen of sweat dampening his skin, and suddenly aching to feel it beneath her fingertips.

He must have registered her sudden surge of need, because he made a sound deep in his throat and lifted her hand to his chest, his eyes never leaving hers.

'You made me hurt, Bea, and only you can take that pain away.' He raised his other hand and unfastened the buttons on his shirt, still holding her gaze.

Beatrice could feel her heart pumping. She could feel her body reacting to him. Breathless and dazed, she lay completely still as he placed her hand over the hard flesh above his heart.

'Feel... feel what you do to me,' he groaned, holding her hand against the shallow intense thud of his heartbeat, making her measure its betraying trip. 'I'm no actor, Beatrice. I can't pretend or fake what I don't feel.'

She looked at him, hardly daring to believe what her senses were telling her.

'*Why*? *Why* did you run away from me? Was it really because you don't want me?'

She felt herself sigh, a long shuddering sound of release and maturity. 'No... No. It was because I love you and because I was afraid.'

How easy it was to make the admission, and he made it easy for her, she recognised gratefully as his mouth came down on hers, silencing any further explanations.

'Italian men seem to like curvy women.' She made the comment in an abstracted little voice for no apparent reason. Immediately she saw a glitter of possessiveness lighten Elliott's eyes.

'They aren't the only ones,' he told her lightly. His hand had moved beneath the waistband of her skirt and her blouse and was caressing the indentation of her waist. 'I want to see you... touch you... make sure that you aren't some figment of my imagination.'

The low, tortured words raised goosebumps on her skin. She shivered slightly, recognising their suppressed passion, still half inclined to disbelieve that Elliott could actually feel so intensely about her.

As though he read her thoughts he said thickly, 'Don't look at me like that! I'm trying as hard as I know how to hold on to my self-control. I want you so much it's tearing me apart. It was bad enough before, when all I could do was imagine what it would be like to make love to you, but now that I actually have...' He closed his eyes in sudden anguish, and Beatrice reached out automatically to touch him, pressing her fingertips against his mouth to silence the groan building deep in his throat.

His hand grasped her wrist, his mouth opening over her fingers, slowly sucking on them until she could feel the sensation he was creating inside her right down to her toes. Her wide darkened eyes betrayed her pleasure and her shock, and as his teeth nipped softly at her smooth flesh he murmured huskily, 'And that's only the start of how I want to make you feel.'

He wasn't making an idle threat, Beatrice acknowledged dazedly later as the sunlight played subtly on their naked bodies, highlighting the difference in texture and tone.

'You learn quickly,' Elliott told her rawly, burying his mouth in her throat. 'Too quickly.' He groaned again, his whole body tensing as he demanded thickly, 'Do you know what you're doing to me?'

She wasn't given the opportunity to answer because his mouth was moving down over her body, its heated demand piercing her with pleasure until she felt she would explode with the sensation building inside her.

Without her realising it, her body arched in wanton appreciation of his touch, deliberately inciting him to claim what she was so enticingly offering.

One hand supported her arched back, the other slid down to cup the rounded curve of her hip. There was too much space between their bodies, she decided fretfully, wrapping her arms round his back and trying to pull him down against her.

'Beatrice...' She heard him groan her name deep in his throat and knew that he wanted her as much as she wanted him.

She woke up slowly, conscious of the most delicious quivers of pleasure running through her, warming her more intensely than the afternoon sun streaming through the window. She moved languorously without opening her eyes, consciousness slowly seeping back.

She opened her eyes, her senses suddenly awake, her mind shocked by the sight of Elliott lying beside her even while her body enjoyed it.

'Now we can talk,' Elliott said quietly.

She nodded, waiting, soothed by his steady tone.

'Ben was trying to frighten you off me. He's always been very possessive where you're concerned. Can't you see that? He never dreamed he'd frighten you to such an extent that you'd run away. Luckily for me he was so distraught when I got back that he admitted the whole thing.'

'But he knew where I was. My note...'

'Your note said only that you were leaving, not where you were going,' Elliott told her patiently. 'It looked as though it had been written in a hurry.'

Guiltily Beatrice remembered her many attempts to write an explanation and the sudden arrival of her taxi while she was in the middle of doing so.

'Luckily it didn't take me long to track you down. Jon's agent was very helpful.'

'You were so angry...' Beatrice shivered.

'You're damned right I was! I came home wanting you... aching for you... and what did I find?'

'I didn't think you cared. I...' Her voice was full of remorse and guilt.

'I realise that. I should have spent more time with you, but I was already committed to going to France.'

'Ben showed me that photograph of you in the paper, and I felt so insecure anyway...'

'Idiot,' he said roughly, 'although Ben's more to blame than you. I'm afraid your brother manoeuvred you very cleverly. You must have realised that he doesn't exactly approve of our relationship.'

'But why?'

'None of your family want to lose you, Bea. They rely too heavily on you, and they certainly don't want to lose you to *me*.'

'But Ben *knew* how I feel about you.' She bit her lip, realising what she was giving away, but apparently Elliott was not surprised by her brother's selfishness.

'Don't think too badly of them. In their shoes I'd have fought just as hard to keep you.'

There was a warning glitter in his eyes that made her pulses flutter. He laughed then.

'Ah, yes, you like the idea of that, don't you? Is that what that secret heart of yours craves, my Bella

Bea . . . a jealous, possessive lover, too hopelessly in
love with you to ever dare to let you go?'

'Isn't that what every woman wants?' she par-
ried lightly.

'Not necessarily.' He smiled humorously at her,
nestling her closer to his warm body, tracing the
half-open shape of her mouth with tender fingers.
'My beautiful Beatrice, who doesn't even know
what she is.'

'What?' she demanded uncertainly.

'The most bewitching, sensual woman in the
world. The only woman I've ever met who can drive
me half out of my mind with just a look. The . . .'

'Oh, Elliott! I'm none of those things.'

'Oh, no?' He looked at her, torn between a groan
and a laugh. 'Didn't it ever strike you that I felt just
as insecure about your feelings as you obviously did
about mine? Put yourself in my shoes, Bea. You
seemed to enjoy my lovemaking, but I couldn't forget how I had lost self-control so much so that I exhausted you physically to the point where you slept
for four hours. In those four hours I had nothing to
do but to go over and over what had happened, and
then when you do wake up, what do you do but turn
away from me, confirming all my fears that I'd
shocked you . . . frightened you off.'

'But you never said anything. You never told me
you loved me or . . .'

He gave an exaggerated sigh. 'Do you know why
not? Because I still wanted you desperately and if
I'd told you that I wouldn't have been able to stop
myself from showing you. I'd wanted you so much
and for so long that once was simply not enough to

appease that need, and that's the truth of the matter,' he finished frankly.

'I've loved you for years, Bea. Almost from the day I saw you, in fact, when I was a teenager and you were little more than a child. Oh, I'm not going to pretend that in those days I knew what my eventual feelings would be—or that I kept myself pure and celibate for you. But there has been a long space of time in my life when I discovered that taking other women to bed simply wasn't the answer, so I stopped doing it.'

'How long?' she asked breathlessly, then flushed as she saw the gleam of light his eyes.

'So long that it's going to be one hell of a long time before I stop wanting to make love to you every time I look at you. Time that can be counted in years, not weeks or months.

'You will marry me won't you?' he demanded abruptly, adding roughly when she nodded her assent, 'and just as quickly as it can be arranged. I'm not going to run the risk of letting your family dissuade you, or of our first child being born too soon. In fact I think we should find ourselves a British Consul and get married before we go home. We could honeymoon here in Italy. What do you think?'

Beatrice opened her mouth to tell him that it was a ridiculously impulsive idea, and to her astonishment heard herself saying huskily,

'I think ... Where is he? The nearest Consul, I mean?'

She heard Elliott laugh, the soft satisfied sound of a man who knows he has got what he wants; it was a sound that punctuated the long afternoon and evening, a silver thread of joy that wove itself round the glittering pleasure of their loving.

Three weeks later they were back in London. After the hectic speed with which Elliott had arranged their wedding, they had spent a week alone in the Fioris' villa, and then another week in Florence as their guests. The combination of love and self-confidence had produced a new Beatrice, who glowed and laughed and who revelled in her femininity with open enjoyment.

Elliott had approved of the subtle changes Lucia had wrought. He liked her new hairstyle and more than appreciated her new clothes.

Lucia had waited only to hear that she was forgiven her interference before embracing the newly married couple, and admitting that it was at her connivance that Carlo had agreed to help Elliott.

'I knew the moment he arrived here on the doorstep, demanding to see Carlo, who he was,' she told Beatrice. 'I saw he loved you, and I knew that you loved him, so...'

They left Italy with regret and many promises to return, and now their taxi was drawing up in front of the Wimbledon house and Beatrice was fighting to control the butterflies running amok in her stomach.

Elliott squeezed her hand reassuringly, and murmured softly,

'It's worse than if we'd run away and were returning to face angry parents, isn't it?'

He was right, and his intuition calmed her. She would never have to stand alone again. She would always have the support and protection of Elliott's love. She knew she ought to be angry with Ben, but her initial sense of outrage had faded, leaving only sadness and the realisation that from now on she was going to have to let her family stand on their own feet.

A period away from them had made her see them more clearly. They were selfish, and not always charmingly so. Mirry and Seb had kinder, gentler natures than the other two, but Lucilla... Her heart ached for the estrangement between her stormy temperamental half-sister and herself. And Ben...Ben who had been able to twist her round his little finger, and who had callously and deliberately tried to keep her and Elliott apart.

Henrietta would not allow them to get away with too much, she told herself comfortingly. Henrietta would take her place here and give them the stability, the retreat, all of them seemed to need.

Henrietta opened the door to them, her frown changing to a smile as she let them in.

The family were gathered in the kitchen and Elliott tucked her arm within his as they walked in.

'So you've found her,' commented Ben, watching them both with narrowed eyes. 'What took you so long?'

Beatrice longed to retort that it was none of her brother's business, but the warning pressure of Elliott's fingers within her own made her stay silent.

'Nothing that you would consider important,' Elliott drawled laconically, his eyes never leaving Ben's taut face. 'Just a small matter of our honeymoon.'

It was Mirry who reacted first, jumping up to rush over and hug them both. No resentment there, Beatrice acknowledged thankfully.

Lucilla turned her back on them both after one bitterly acid look at Beatrice. Sebastian conquered his initial surprise and came over to kiss her and shake Elliott by the hand.

Ben remained exactly where he was.

She wasn't going to coax or cajole him, Beatrice told herself firmly. Her eyes were open now, and she saw her family as they were really were... not minor gods to be protected and cossetted, but human beings like any other... like herself.

'So you let him convince you, did you, Bea?' Ben asked her. There was sadness and pain in his voice, but now Beatrice could see that they were false. She felt anger but suppressed it. In many ways the fault was as much hers as it was Ben's. For too long she had allowed him to manipulate both herself and everyone else around him, until he thought it was his right to dictate her way of life.

Life for all of them was going to have to change. She and Elliott would have their own home, their own life. She looked hard at her brother and said calmly, 'I think that's our business, don't you, Ben?'

He had the grace to look away from her, and for a moment the tension in the room could almost be felt, but then Mirry broke it, nudging William.

'Did you hear, William? Bea and Elliott are married!'

'So what's new?' he demanded with elaborate calmness. 'I knew Elliott would get her in the end.'

'How?' demanded Mirry, scowling at him.

'I've watched him playing chess,' was the oblique reply. 'I suppose we'll have to move away from here now and come and live in the Cotswolds with you?' William addressed the question to Elliott, waiting for his reply, as was everyone else in the room.

She and Elliott had discussed this at great length, and now Beatrice waited tensely for their reaction to what Elliott had to tell them. Mingled with her tension was a sense of release and freedom. From now on, with the exception of William, her siblings would have to learn to fend for themselves, and in all honesty she had to admit that to do so would not do them any harm.

'Not necessarily,' Elliott was saying. 'Beatrice and I are quite prepared to make our home here until you finish school. After that ... well, if Henry wants to stay on and look after the lot of you, then that's up to her, but let's hope by then Beatrice will have—er—responsibilities of her own, which will mean that you lot can cease looking upon her as a surrogate mother.'

'You mean babies,' said William in disgust, ignoring the looks his sister and her husband were exchanging.

'There, that wasn't too bad, was it?' Elliott asked later when he and Beatrice were alone in their room. 'And William only has another six months or so at school. That will give you plenty of time to make whatever alterations you like to the Cotswold house.'

'Did you really mean what you said about keeping this place on and paying Henry to look after them?' Beatrice asked her new husband dreamily.

'I'm not being as altruistic as it sounds. That way I don't get them descending on us for long rests between productions. I'm a selfish man, Bea, just as selfish as the rest of your family, and I want you all to myself . . . at least for the next year or so.'

'It might already be too late,' Beatrice reminded him demurely. 'How do you think you'll take to being a father?'

He cut off her teasing words with the warm pressure of his mouth.

Downstairs Sebastian looked sympathetically at his twin and said reasonably, 'Come on, Ben, you must have known you couldn't win. You got rid of the others easily enough, but Elliott was a different proposition, and she's happy with him. We couldn't have held on to her for ever, you know. I've been given a couple of free tickets for the new production. Want to come with me?'

'Why not?' Ben agreed lazily. 'After all, there's nothing to keep me here.'

Upstairs Elliott looked tenderly into Beatrice's eyes.

'He'll get over it, you know. He's young and arrogant and in the long run it will do him good to know that he can't win every time, and I promise you I won't rub it in.'

'You're being very generous, Elliott. When I think of how easily . . .'

'Shush! That's all over now, and as for being generous, I can afford to be. I've got you.'

'For always,' she breathed against his mouth.

His arms tightened possessively around her.

'It'd better be, because I'll never willingly let you go.'

Masquerade Historical Romances

Life and love in the past

Masquerade Historical Romances, published by Mills & Boon, vividly recreate the past. Picture the days of real romance – from the colourful courts of mediaeval Spain to the studied manners of Regency England, secret assignations and high intrigue – all are portrayed with authentic historical backgrounds. Look out for this exciting series. Two superb new stories are published each month.

Buy them from your usual paperback stockist, or write to: Mills & Boon Reader Service, P.O. Box 236, Thornton Rd, Croydon, Surrey CR9 3RU, England. Readers in South Africa-write to: Independent Book Services Pty, Postbag X3010, Randburg 2125, S. Africa.

Mills & Boon
the rose of romance

Doctor Nurse Romances

Romance in the dedicated world of medicine

Behind the scenes of modern medical life, where emotional pressure is intense, doctors and nurses often find romance. Read about their lives and loves set against the fascinatingly different backgrounds of contemporary medicine – hospitals, country practices, health clinics – wherever help is needed. Each month, the three Mills & Boon Doctor Nurse Romances offer tremendous variety.

Buy them from your usual paperback stockist, or write to: Mills & Boon Reader Service, P.O. Box 236, Thornton Rd, Croydon, Surrey CR9 3RU, England. Readers in South Africa-write to: Independent Book Services Pty, Postbag X3010, Randburg 2125, S. Africa.

Mills & Boon
the rose of romance